ALMOST CRIMINAL

ALMOST CRIMINAL

A NOVEL

ULRIKE HERWIG

Translated by Rachel Reynolds

Previously published as *Oskar an Bord* by dtv in Germany in 2015. Translated from German by Rachel Reynolds. First published in English by Amazon Crossing in 2026.

Published by Amazon Crossing, Seattle

www.apub.com

EU product safety contact:
Amazon Media EU S. à r.l.
38, avenue John F. Kennedy, L-1855 Luxembourg
amazonpublishing-gpsr@amazon.com

ISBN-13: 9781662535222 (paperback)
ISBN-13: 9781662535215 (digital)

Cover illustration and design by Philip Pascuzzo

Printed in the United States of America

ALMOST CRIMINAL

1

The day started out as a run-of-the-mill bad day but soon escalated into one of catastrophic proportions.

That morning, Tina had discovered that their joint account was once again overdrawn, and they would have to muddle through an entire week until the next paycheck. The fight with Markus had careened off the rails, and the mere thought of the coming week, bleak and full of noodles and ketchup and long faces, made her want to instantly bolt for Australia. *By herself.* But, of course, she lacked the funds for that.

Her hopelessly dull job at the Fashion World catalog did nothing to improve her mood. Quite the opposite, truth be told. Especially in light of the fact that Tina was forfeiting most of her valuable lunchtime because half of her coworkers were out sick, and some indecisive customer on the phone couldn't make up her mind whether she wanted to order the Bermuda shorts, size XXL, in hot pink or chestnut brown. It was a pointless debate, in Tina's opinion, since she considered them both hideous options.

She glanced over at her coworker Marion, who was sitting at the neighboring desk, halfheartedly flipping through a catalog. "Do you mean the corduroy blazer in chartreuse?" Tina heard her ask into the phone.

Tina almost broke out laughing. She and Marion had voted the corduroy blazer in chartreuse their absolute least favorite item in the spring collection. Anyone who wore it would end up looking like SpongeBob.

Marion caught Tina's eyes and rolled her own. In response, Tina pantomimed choking herself. They grinned at each other. At least Tina had one kindred spirit in this dump.

"I don't know." Tina's customer now sighed on the other end of the line. "The chestnut brown is stylish, but the hot pink isn't bad either. What do *you* think?"

"Both shorts are classy and very pretty." Fingers drumming.

"Well . . . hmm."

"Would you like to give this some more thought and call back later?" Tina suggested, as accommodating as possible. "Maybe grab some lunch"—this was as broad a hint as she could make—"and call back in an hour or so, Ms. . . ." Tina glanced at the customer number on her screen. What was her name, anyway?

On the other end of the line, the customer fell into consternated silence. Then the voice resumed, this time unmistakably insulted. "Scheller. *Mr.* Scheller."

Oops!

"Oh, I . . ." Tina gulped as a thousand excuses raced through her mind, but none of them were viable. So, she decided to commit the gravest mortal sin of any customer service employee: She simply hung up.

Luckily, her boss didn't notice anything because she was in the process of picking on poor Marion, so Tina snatched up her purse and fled out into the free, fresh air, even though it was already in the eighties in the shade, unusual for Ingolstadt, a town in Bavaria—a state in the southern part of Germany. She wanted to go to her regular baker to indulge in the one good thing this day could still offer: a crunchy ciabatta sandwich with arugula, tomato, and mozzarella. For ten minutes, the pleasure of consuming this sandwich would transport Tina to a parallel universe. To Italy, to a balmy, carefree life full of olive groves and basil, in a white cottage with a cool sea breeze and . . .

She stopped in front of the bakery, reading the handwritten sign outside in disbelief. Suddenly, the ciabatta sandwiches were 4.50 euros apiece. Had they been brushed with liquid gold, or was this some kind of joke? Why did everything seem to get pricier by the hour? Dammit! The only other place around that carried food was the gas station down the street.

"Got a euro?" a voice to her left begged. "For Morli, my cat?" The crazy old woman with the straw hat had materialized next to Tina.

She lived in one of the nearby supervised care homes and spent the whole day wandering the streets, carrying her cat around in a beach bag. *No, I don't* was on the tip of Tina's tongue. *To be precise, I have five euros to my name, and they are for two sandwiches and two drinks, for today and tomorrow. If that's even enough, considering how expensive stuff is at the gas station.*

"Morli is hungry." The old woman's clothes were astonishingly thick for the time of year, and she smelled. She had pink cheeks like a child and was petting her cat.

Tina hesitated for a moment, then handed the woman a euro. "Of course. Here you go."

On such an awful day as this, nothing really mattered anyway. *At least I haven't completely lost my mind, wandering around in high summer with a straw hat, a fur vest, and a cat.* She was grateful for the little things.

"Thank you, dear. You'll get that back a thousand times over!" the old woman exclaimed with a toothless smile.

Tina smiled indulgently in return. She would welcome a euro that came back to her with a thousand siblings. No question about that. First, she'd settle all those cursed bills, then treat herself to something nice—and if there was still enough left, she'd give a little to someone worse off than she was, though that bar wasn't exactly set high. What was it they said about good karma? *All good things come around again?*

An Audi R8 promptly sped past them and sprayed Tina with puddle water, one final greeting from the ridiculously brief storm the night before. A young man, not much older than Tina's son Paul, was sitting at the wheel of the car. She stared after him, stunned. How could the world be like this? How could a young person with such bad manners have so much money, while Tina and Markus, despite their annoying full-time jobs, could never get ahead? The young people were probably dealing drugs. How else could they get their hands on so much money? Just recently, a ninth-grade kid at Paul's school had been arrested for grinding up his autism medication and selling it at a premium as crack to his classmates. *That much chutzpah and entrepreneurial spirit is almost admirable,* Tina thought. Sometimes there were things that could be learned from the younger generation. With the remaining four euros clutched tightly in her hand, she sighed and marched off toward the gas station.

~

The sallow neon light gave the station the cozy ambience of a morgue, an impression intensified by the cashier in a yellow apron who was dozing, open mouthed, behind the register. Tina looked around. Obviously the product in highest demand among drivers was beer, closely followed by sunglasses and greeting cards featuring Diddl Mouse.

Besides Tina, there were a few other people in the gas station. One man was wearing the ugliest glasses she had ever seen, a kind of orthopedic shoe for the face. He frowned as he openly read a newspaper he hadn't paid for. Next to him, two young men in athletic pants and undershirts were expertly eyeing a pyramid of beer cans, and a woman around Tina's age with dark rings under her eyes was sipping coffee from a paper cup in the grandiosely named Bistro Corner.

Enjoy yourself again, a poster bearing a chocolate ad mocked everyone in the store. Tina walked over to the bistro corner and studied the pathetic sandwiches, which probably had the nutritional value of a pot holder despite the few lettuce leaves peeking out coyly. The wilted pieces were quite expensive to boot. But what other options did she have? Coffee to go and a soggy croissant? Or a bag of trail mix? Tina trudged aimlessly around the dim shop. Whatever. At least it was cool in here. She would simply sit down next to the woman with the rings under her eyes and stare at the wall for the remaining forty minutes of her lunch break, just like the other woman was doing. If someone took a black-and-white picture of them, it would qualify as art. If it didn't, the photo would simply be a snapshot of what a shitty life looked like.

The guys in the undershirts were now paying, and outside, an ambulance pulled up to a pump. The door jingled as someone stepped inside. Tina turned away. If she bought only a small bag of peanuts, she could afford a tabloid paper and lose herself temporarily in the lives of the rich and famous. It would help her forget about her own. She reached out longingly for one of the splashy magazines. Lose 5 kilos by tomorrow! Brad and Angelina still aren't divorced yet! Madonna is actually 78 years old! How to finally get your life under control!

A small cry came from the direction of the cash register. "Oh no!"

Had something fallen? Tina couldn't see anything except the woman with the dark rings under her eyes, who was now covering her mouth in horror. The man with the orthopedic glasses had dropped his newspaper and put his hands up. What was going on?

"All of it. In there, make it fast!" a man's voice ordered.

A holdup! Tina started to tremble. She couldn't see the culprit, though, because the shelves blocked her line of sight. However, that didn't mean he hadn't noticed her.

"Please point the gun somewhere else. I'm doing it!" The cashier was now sobbing.

The guy was armed—oh God! Tina ducked down and hid behind the candy display, wishing she could crawl inside a box of gummy bears.

"Hurry up!" the voice commanded again.

Something about the voice struck Tina as familiar. Could it be someone she . . . ? Tina glanced up cautiously at the large mirror on the ceiling, which was mounted in such a way that you could see the entire store. What she saw made her gasp. This couldn't be happening. No—surely not . . . She crouched, frozen, stunned, unable to move or respond. The man standing at the counter and holding a pistol in his right hand, trained on the ashen cashier—the man in the striped casual shirt that was always so hard to get ironed, the man with the frantic look, the armed, ice-cold culprit—was none other than Tina's own husband, Markus. According to all rules of reason, he was supposed to be restocking shelves at the supermarket where he was in charge of stuff like beverages and cornflakes and shampoo.

"Markus?" Tina whispered in confusion. "What in the world are you doing?"

Of course, he couldn't hear her. He didn't seem to be registering anything except the bundle of bills that the cashier was throwing into the open Aldi bag. Only a few days ago, Tina had used that very bag to carry home butter, laundry detergent, and cottage cheese, and now Markus was using it for an armed robbery. Had he lost his last bit of sanity at that stupid supermarket, somewhere among the frozen peas and the bathroom cleansers? Tina stood up reluctantly.

"Get down!" the other woman hissed in horror, but Tina ignored her.

"That's all there is," the cashier insisted pleadingly, pointing at the empty drawer. "Honestly, I swear!" The woman had started hiccupping in all her panic.

Markus spun around abruptly and strode toward the door. "No police, got it?" he shouted back over his shoulder.

"All right, I . . . well . . . shit . . ." The shocked cashier was gripping the empty cash register tightly as the door swung shut behind Markus. Tina raced after him.

"Stay here, don't be stupid!" the cashier shouted. "He's armed!"

"That's my husband!" Tina yelled back.

"Someone call the police," the man with the glasses croaked from his corner.

Tina pushed open the outside door, the packet of peanuts still in her hand. Whatever. But where was Markus? Where was his car? He was nowhere to be seen. The only vehicle outside was the ambulance whose mustached driver was just screwing on the gas cap. Somebody gave him a shove. Markus.

"Scram! Get out of here!" Markus waved his pistol in the face of the astonished driver, who let himself be pushed aside. In one fluid movement, Markus swung himself into the driver's seat and started the engine. And with another fluid movement, Tina yanked open the passenger door. "Markus! Have you lost your mind?"

"Tina." Markus stared at her as if the ghost of Hamlet's father had suddenly materialized among the gas pumps. "What . . . Why are you . . . ?"

"Police!" somebody shouted. "Help! Robbery!"

"Come on." Markus leaned over and hauled Tina into the passenger seat. "We have to get the hell out of here. Hurry and shut the door!"

Later on, Tina couldn't have said why she did what she did. Maybe it was the sight of the woman with the dark circles under her eyes and the lukewarm coffee that had so perfectly mirrored Tina's own dismal existence. Maybe it was the frustration she'd felt over the unobtainable ciabatta sandwich. Maybe it was fear related to the complaint *Mr.* Scheller would probably lodge that afternoon. Maybe it was just reflex. Whatever it was, she climbed in.

Markus revved the engine, shifted into first gear, and tore off like a madman. In the distance, police sirens started to howl.

2

For a few seconds, neither of them said a word, and then they both started talking at once.

"Markus, you've lost your mind. You've obviously completely lost your mind. I—"

"I can explain everything, Tina. I swear I didn't mean to hurt anyone. I swear!"

Tina took a deep breath. "Where did you get the pistol? Who sold it to you?"

Markus avoided making eye contact. "More Than Just Balls."

"What?"

"It's from More Than Just Balls."

"Are you serious? Markus, that isn't even funny. What do you mean?"

"More Than Just Balls. The toy shop down on the square, dammit." Markus barely managed to miss an oncoming truck barreling down the narrow street. "Crap!"

"A toy gun?"

"Of course, what do you think? That I'd run around with a real one?! I'm not crazy."

"That's not what it looks like. At the moment, you're acting pretty crazy. Wait, do you hear that?" Tina opened her window; police sirens were still wailing in the distance. "Do you hear that? They're coming to get you."

"To get *us*. You're involved, too, you know."

Tina opened her mouth to protest, but then it dawned on her that Markus was right. She was involved. The salesclerk would give her witness statement and tell the police that there was a second suspect, a woman, who had been hanging around the shop, probably to keep the other people under control. And then, after the successful robbery, she had immediately jumped in the van with the burglar after claiming he was her husband. And she had stolen the peanuts as well! Tina angrily hurled the nuts onto the floorboard. What was the saying? In for a penny, in for a pound. For God's sake, how could Markus do this to her? He had developed a few strange quirks recently, such as his obsession with the idea of breeding and selling koi fish (end result: five dead giant fish in their bathtub) and tramping across the fields on Sundays with his metal detector in search of old coins (end result: countless bottle caps and soft drink tabs, in addition to two dental caps). But this surpassed everything else. On top of it all, he was now racing at least twenty miles above the speed limit.

"Slow down!" she shouted angrily. "Do you want to get us killed? Or arrested? Or both?"

Markus slammed on the brakes, and the van lurched. Tina held on for dear life.

"Shit!" he cursed. "Since when has there been a detour here?"

"Where do you want to go? Do you mind sharing that with me? Perhaps somewhere like home?" Tina forced her voice to remain calm, but all she could produce was a stressed squeak.

Home. Half of their fellow residents would be sitting on their balconies by now, eagerly watching everything happening down on the street. An ambulance rushing up at breakneck speed and the Michels barreling out of it with an Aldi bag full of cash would be a welcome change to the never-ending parade of geraniums and trash cans and mail carriers.

"We need to get out of town," Markus replied, glancing nervously left and right before speeding through the intersection. "Thank goodness the gas tank is full."

The tank was full, marvelous. Then everything was just grand. Tina gave a short, hysterical snort. "I can't believe it. Then what?"

"No idea! It wasn't like I planned this. I didn't plan anything. I did it on the fly, all right? I was just fed up with everything. And you kept going on and on about how broke we were, and then that thing with the car—" He broke off and, to Tina's dismay, hastily wiped his eyes.

"What about the car? Markus?" Tina placed a hand on his arm.

"Junk metal. That's what it is. Totaled. I hit a streetlight because I was staring at my phone. Now you know. My phone went off, and I thought it might be a text from the company I applied to last week. Because my store is about to be bought out. By Aldi, of all companies!" He gave the innocent plastic bag on Tina's lap an angry poke.

"But . . . Just a minute. I don't understand." Tina pressed her fingertips to her temples. The heat, the sirens wailing outside, Markus's incredible confession. It was all too much. "Okay, you were in an accident. Not nice, but it happens. That's why we have insurance. You don't hold up a gas station because of that."

"We don't have any insurance. I stopped paying that bill a few months ago." Markus stared ahead stubbornly. He then turned down a country road that led out of town. "Do you finally get it, Tina? We can't pay for the repairs or for the streetlight either. We no longer have a car, and we have no insurance. Got it?"

"We have no insurance," Tina repeated dully. This had to be a joke. Some idiotic, silly joke. Any second, Markus would park the van, pull on a jester's cap with bells, and shout "April Fools'!" despite the fact it was the middle of July.

"And . . . was the text about the job?" Tina asked. It was the only thing she could think of at the moment.

"No." Markus pressed his lips together. "The text was from Mr. Umgabe Arando from Nigeria, my good friend, believe it or not, who informed me in broken German that he would like to temporarily transfer a million euros into my account and needs my account number for the transaction."

"Umgabe Arando." Tina pressed her fingers even harder against her temples. She longed to bury her face in her hands and submerge herself in the pleasantly empty darkness in which there were no crazy husbands, gas stations, totaled cars, or robberies. Speaking of which . . . "How much did you actually get off that poor cashier?"

"No clue. Take a look. I . . . Shit. They're getting closer." The police sirens really did sound like they were getting louder. "I'm going to take a shortcut." Markus yanked the steering wheel to the side and made a spontaneous decision to drive down a dusty road full of potholes. "This goes past the Auwaldsee Lake, I think. We'll be able to catch the A9 on the other side of it, which'll be perfect."

"Then what?" Tina asked again. "Have you forgotten that Paul will be home in two hours? And at some point, he'll wonder where his parents are."

"No, he won't. He couldn't care less if we aren't around."

"How can you say that?"

"Okay—if *I'm* not around. I know exactly what he thinks of me. How much is in there?"

Tina angrily grabbed the plastic bag of bills and coins, which was being jostled around by the bumpy road. "Wait. Don't drive so fast. I won't be able to keep hold of it. Umm . . . They're almost all tens and fives. Fifty, hundred, two hundred, five hundred . . ."

"Watch out." Markus barely dodged a hole in the road that looked like a comet could have made it. "There are some trees up ahead, and I'll pull over. Nobody'll be able to see us."

Tina didn't reply. She concentrated on the bills, because counting bills demanded attentiveness and allowed no time for wildly fluttering, panicked thoughts.

"Eight hundred and thirty-four euros," she said at the same moment Markus slammed on the brakes and came to a stop at the edge of the woods. "She slipped a bunch of coins in there too."

The words she'd used, *She slipped a bunch of coins in there too,* made it sound as if the terrified cashier was her dear old Aunt Dora, who'd always given her a few coins for her piggy bank when she was a kid. Now that the ambulance had stopped moving, Tina felt nauseous all of a sudden. What had they done?

"Shit," Markus whispered. "That's it?"

"What do you mean, *that's it*? You know that the police don't care how much is taken in a robbery, right? Armed robbery is armed robbery, and—"

"Hello?" a soft voice suddenly called out from somewhere behind them.

Tina froze. "What was that?"

Markus looked at her in bewilderment.

"Hello?" the voice called again, this time a little louder. "I need to get out for a moment, please."

"It's coming from the back of the ambulance," Markus whispered.

"Do you think there's somebody *back there*?"

"Sounds like it."

"Hello?" the voice came again. "It really is a little urgent."

"Oh God, I can't believe it. I simply can't believe it." Tina resisted the temptation to run into the woods and scream at the top of her lungs.

She and Markus turned around at the same time. Behind them was the partition between the driver and transport spaces, which Tina had been too distracted to notice. On the right side, she discovered an adjustable red stretcher, to which several straps were attached. The stretcher was empty. But on the other side of the space sat a wheelchair, which was also secured with a strap. And someone was sitting in that. A little old man with a bald head, except for the white strip of hair that curled around his head like a laurel wreath. He was wearing blue corduroy pants, a red checkered shirt, and fuzzy light-brown slippers.

"Well, clearly my beauty has left you speechless. And yes, I'm happy to sign an autograph—but first, nature is calling rather urgently." The old man chuckled.

3

"Do something!" Tina hissed.

"What should I do?" Markus hissed back.

Tina rolled her eyes, got out of the van, slammed the passenger door shut, and walked around the ambulance. She could hear Markus getting out too. She jerked open the back door.

"Well, that took you long enough," the old man declared.

"We . . ." Tina started, but for the life of her, she couldn't think of anything else to say.

"I know, you kidnapped me." The old man waved this off with a smile. "But you still need to let me pee. That's a basic human right. We'll eventually become friends, and then we'll have an actual case of Stockholm syndrome on our hands."

"What?" Tina stared at the old man. What was he talking about?

"Pull out the ramp, my boy." The old man now turned to Markus, who had come to a paralyzed halt behind Tina. "Then roll my chair down, and take me back to that clearing over there. I can get out of this thing myself and can walk a little. And luckily I can still take care of business on my own." He grinned.

Tina and Markus silently set to fulfilling the old man's wish. Markus pulled out the ramp and pushed the chair out of the ambulance. Tina rolled the old man to the spot he had pointed out and watched him slowly make his way through the clearing, before discreetly turning around and hurrying back to Markus.

"Should we just drive off real fast?" Markus asked quietly.

"Of course not. Do you want to have both robbery and murder on your conscience? He wouldn't last a day in these woods."

"Yes, but what do you want to do with him? He's got to be almost a hundred."

"Eighty-seven," the old man replied from the edge of the trees. "And my hearing is still tip-top. My legs are the only thing that don't work so well anymore. But I'm glad you don't want to murder me."

Markus bit his lip.

"He heard everything," Tina whispered in horror. "The whole robbery."

"Done!" the old man exclaimed cheerfully.

This time, Markus retrieved the man in the wheelchair, pushed him back into the ambulance, and strapped him in.

"What exactly are you planning to do next?" the old man inquired. "Did you knock out my driver? I didn't quite catch that part, unfortunately."

"No." Markus shot Tina a shocked glance.

"Really? That would've done him some good. He always shouted so loudly and talked so slowly, as if I were senile and couldn't hear a thing. But it's all still there." The old man patted his head proudly.

"What's your name?" Tina asked. The fresh air was gradually reenergizing her brain.

"Oskar Krauss. Krauss with a double *s*. But just call me Oskar. It looks like we'll be spending a little time together. My lousy son-in-law definitely won't pay any ransom money for me. I should tell you that right now. He'll just be glad to be rid of me. He won't even pay the cost of the Sonnenberg Assisted Living Community and would rather ship me off to a nursing home called Luisenhaus because it's cheaper." The old man called Oskar gave a disdainful grunt. "It's awful there. It reeks of pea soup, floor wax, and diapers, and everyone is knocking on heaven's door, if you know what I mean. At least they had cable TV at

Sonnenberg, and the nurses were cute, even if they were usually in a bad mood and—"

"We didn't mean to kidnap you," Tina interrupted. Her head was buzzing. Why wasn't Markus doing anything? Earlier he'd pretended to be the tough gangster, but now he was just standing there in his silly leisure shirt, with his arms dangling uselessly at his sides and a look on his face that reminded her of one of his idiotic koi fish.

"Sure." Oskar gave her a complicit wink. "Never share your actual plans with your prisoner! You want him to think he's safe, so he doesn't go crazy on you. I know how this works. So what should I call you? Bonnie and Clyde?"

"One moment, please," Tina murmured as she shut the back door. "Follow me." She motioned to Markus and pointed at a deer stand about fifty yards away. The strange old man wouldn't be able to hear them up there.

They tiptoed away, cautiously scanning their surroundings. There was no one in sight.

"If you have something to drink, that wouldn't be bad either," the old man's voice called out from the van. "It's pretty hot back here, and my circulation is sometimes spotty. I wouldn't be much use to you dehydrated and dead, would I?" A raspy chuckle punctuated this commentary.

Tina leaned back against the ladder to the deer stand, wiped her forehead, and quickly pulled her long dark hair back into a ponytail. It was blazing hot. Today of all days, she had put on a long-sleeved black blouse, because the air conditioning in her office was always set to arctic temperatures. Speaking of the office, she really needed to call Marion and tell her that she probably wouldn't make it back to the office this afternoon. Her boss would be furious, but Tina couldn't care about that right now. There were certain things here that needed to be . . . clarified.

Markus stood in front of her and nervously cracked his knuckles. Sweat rings were spreading under his armpits, his glasses were askew, and his brown hair was clinging to his forehead, giving him the air of a slightly nutty professor.

"This is all your fault!" Tina snapped, anger bubbling inside her, ready to erupt like a volcano at any moment. "Do you ever stop to think? About anything? We're monumentally screwed, and it's all because of you! And stop cracking your knuckles. You know that sound drives me bonkers."

"Okay, okay. The old man thinks we meant to kidnap him, and for some reason, he's actually happy about that. He is obviously completely senile. That's a good thing for us."

"Why?"

"Because nobody will take him seriously. For instance, when he tells the police about us. He's seen our faces, don't forget that."

Tina frowned and shook her head. "Markus, *everyone* at the gas station saw our faces. Our faces are on the surveillance cameras too. They don't actually need that old man's statement. But he's still a problem for us, since the police will think we kidnapped him. So now we're talking about robbery *and* kidnapping. Do you even know what that means? How you've messed up our lives with this insanely stupid act?"

"I . . ." he croaked, but she wasn't finished yet.

"I'll tell you what it means, because you clearly haven't given it any thought. It means ten years in jail, at the very least. Ten years of mushy peas and sadistic fellow inmates and toilets in the corners of our cells, where everyone can watch you, and if you're lucky, a job in the prison laundry, and . . ." Her voice faltered as tears trickled down her cheeks. "And that's all thanks to you!"

"That's ridiculous. You're thinking about that documentary we watched a few days ago about Alcatraz. These days, jail cells have Wi-Fi. At least, I think they do." As he said this, Markus couldn't look her in the eyes.

"Great. That means I'll be able to update my Facebook status from prison. *This morning I was beaten to a pulp by gang members.*" Tina gave a scornful sniff. She glanced over at the ambulance, which had fallen completely silent. What if the old man had had a heart attack? Crap.

"We have to get out of here," Tina said. "We'll drive to the next town and drop him off so that somebody will find him right away. Then he'll be taken care of, and we won't have to deal with him anymore."

"Good idea," Markus agreed immediately. He seemed relieved that she had made the decision. "And then—"

Tina cut him off. "Then we'll see." They first needed to ditch this kidnapping-obsessed grandpa. They couldn't make any sensible decisions as long as he was sitting in the back of the ambulance.

~

NIEDERFELD, announced a yellow town sign, which looked a little worse for wear and was leaning at a slant on the edge of the village. The first sight of Niederfeld wasn't exactly heartening: a lonesome, dusty main street; snug little houses lining both sides of the road; a cat on a wall; a weathered sign pointing toward a business park; a small church; and a mail truck. In the distance, a lawnmower roared.

"What a wretched dump!" a voice exclaimed from the back.

Tina still flinched involuntarily every time the voice came out of nowhere. Like the Phantom of the Opera, the old man in the wheelchair was lurking there in the back. Tina didn't think he looked all that weak or withered up. Unlike her and Markus. She was practically dying of thirst by this point. To distract herself, she pulled out her phone and dialed the number for Fashion World.

"Fashion World—everything for women. My name is Ms. Müller. What can I do for you?" a voice rang out. Tina recognized chubby Müller, the boss's snitch and spy. She was the last person Tina wanted to talk to.

"I have a complaint that Ms. Walter was working on. Could you please put me through to her?" Tina disguised her voice as best she could. Müller was lazy by nature and wouldn't mind passing a complaint on to someone else. Shortly afterward, Marion picked up the phone, clearly irritated.

"Hello, this is Ms. Walter."

"It's me," Tina whispered. "I'm in trouble."

"At Fashion World, we can easily take care of your troubles. Could you please give me your customer number?"

"Marion!" Tina hissed a little louder. "This is Tina!"

"Tina? Okay. What is your last name?"

"Good grief, it's me! Tina. Haven't you noticed that I'm not sitting in my seat?" Sometimes Marion's cluelessness really was tiresome. And now she had obviously lost her ability to string thoughts together lucidly.

"Tina? Hi! It's so noisy here, and the connection is really bad . . . You're right. You actually aren't here. Where are you?"

"I am . . . Listen, Marion, tell the boss that I probably won't be back this weekend." Tina lowered her voice. "I'm in an ambulance, and we—"

"What? An ambulance? I can't really hear you. Are you sick?"

"Well . . . we . . . I mean, I . . ." It was crackling horribly on the line. "I'm on the run!" Tina exclaimed. "The police are after us."

"The coppers," the old man corrected her loudly from the rear.

"Who was that?" Marion asked in confusion. "And why are the cops after you? Who else is with you? You just wanted to go to the bakery, didn't you?"

"Marion, I can't explain right now. Just tell *her* that I won't be back in today."

"The corduroy blazer in magenta? Let me see if we still have it in stock." Marion's voice abruptly became businesslike, from which Tina could deduce that their boss was standing right behind her.

"I'll call back later," Tina said hurriedly and hung up.

"Ah, the boss. Well now." The grandpa's voice came from the back again. "Is she the one behind all this? Respect. Female mobsters are obviously on the rise."

"Could you please just . . . ?" Tina clenched the fabric of her pants and bit her lip. There was no point in arguing with this obviously completely confused old man. She fell wearily silent, and for a while, nobody said anything.

"Zombie town," Markus eventually murmured as they drove through the town at walking speed. "Where is everyone?"

"There are a few people over there." Tina pointed at two women with shopping bags, who were chatting on the edge of the street while staring at the ambulance with curiosity. "They've been shopping, so there has to be a store nearby. Let's find it, and set him out there."

"No way!" the old man in the back suddenly shouted. "I'm not staying here."

"Mr. Krauss, it's for your own good," Tina declared in a firm voice. She practically felt like a nurse.

"Call me Oskar. And it'll be for my own good? Don't make me laugh. What's good for me is stuff like—"

"Over there," Tina interrupted him. She had decided to ignore the old man. "Markus, there's a shop."

Something that halfway deserved to be called a store had just appeared up ahead of them. A blackboard sidewalk sign on which someone had scribbled FRESH EGGS stood in front of it. Fruit was rotting away in crates beside the door, and a bike was waiting for its owner. Markus stopped the ambulance a short distance from the business and briefly checked the road in the rearview mirror.

"No one in sight. Good. Let's go!" He got out of the car.

Tina immediately followed him. "Perhaps we should place an anonymous call to the Red Cross," she suggested quietly as Markus opened the rear door and slid out the ramp. "They could pick him up and take him straight to that nursing home."

"I don't want to get out," the old man grumbled as Markus climbed into the ambulance, unbuckled the straps, and pushed the wheelchair down the ramp. "Forget it. Do you know what it's like there? Nothing but drowsy old geezers whose dentures keep falling out. They wet their beds and think they're Marlene Dietrich!" His voice grew louder and louder.

"Just be quiet!" Tina looked around frantically. Through the shop window, she could see a salesclerk and a customer chatting together. The two women then fell silent and turned toward them.

"I'll talk as loud as I want," the old man exclaimed, standing his ground. "And I'll also say what I want. For example . . . Help! Help! I'm being kidnapped! Help!"

The two women in the shop, now curious, walked over to the exit and onto the sidewalk. "What are you doing?" one of them called out, hands on her hips.

Markus was so startled that he almost tipped the old man out of his chair.

"Help!!" the old man shouted even louder.

"Mr. Krauss, stop that!" Tina hissed furiously. Somewhere a door banged, a dog barked, and a car drew closer down the main road.

The two women approached slowly. "What are you doing to that man?" one of them asked.

"Kidnapping!" the old man bellowed. "People of this town, help a man cast down!"

"Advanced . . . accutitis," Tina called, hoping that sounded serious. "Final stage. At this point, they talk crazy and lash out and might accidentally kill people. That's how my grandmother's doctor died. Please, don't come any closer!"

The two women stopped and exchanged uncertain looks.

"Kidnapping!" Oskar yelled again.

"Don't listen to him. He has no idea what he's saying." Tina turned her back on the gawking women and hissed, "Mr. Krauss . . . Oskar! Stop it. Please."

Oskar instantly fell silent. A tiny smile flitted across his wrinkled face. "You said *Oskar* and *please* very nicely. And now we just need to get out of here before the village idiots smell a rat."

Tina's thoughts whizzed frantically back and forth through her head. What should they do now? The women had started whispering.

One of them pulled out her phone, and the approaching car was a few hundred yards away.

"Markus, push him back inside." Tina made a quick decision. "Let's get out of here. With Oskar."

"But . . ." Markus blinked in confusion and stood frozen where he was.

"Come on." Tina grabbed the wheelchair by the handles herself, swung it around, and pushed the old man back into the ambulance. She hurriedly tightened the straps. If you wanted something done right, you had to do it yourself.

"Thanks, sweetie," Oskar croaked, sounding cheerful.

Tina didn't respond. She slammed the door shut and gave Markus, who obviously still hadn't grasped what was going on, a shove.

"Come on." Tina pulled him by the sleeve.

Markus started the ambulance as the woman began to speak excitedly into her phone and the unfamiliar car got within twenty yards of them.

"Crap." In a fit of wild desperation, Tina switched on the ambulance siren. It began screeching, and the car behind them slammed on its brakes as the two women from the shop whipped their heads around.

"Marvelous!" Oscar cheered from the rear. "I've always wanted to do that."

Markus thundered down the main street, his eyes glued straight ahead. It wasn't until they had put half a mile between themselves and Niederfeld that he slowed down and finally turned off the siren. He pulled up beneath a cherry tree on the edge of the road. "Time for plan B, right? Do we even have a plan B?"

"Nope," Oskar declared from the back. "Time for plan O. *O* for Oskar." A hoarse chortle followed. "Now listen to me, you two crooks. Our kind has to stick together, don't we?"

"Our kind?" Turning around, Tina studied the old man, who was in the process of kicking off his fuzzy slippers. Striped knitted socks now appeared.

Oskar pulled these off as well. "Boy, do my corns hurt! You don't happen to have any corn bandages, do you?"

"No, we don't." Tina took a deep breath. "Oskar, what did you mean . . . what did you mean when you said *our kind*?"

Oskar winked at her. "Birds of a feather and all that. I used to be young once, too, you know? Though I never pulled off a robbery. Kudos to you! But your planning isn't up to snuff. It really isn't. You're fluttering around like drunken May beetles."

He isn't wrong about that, Tina thought. But what did he want from them? Who *was* this?

Markus cleared his throat. "What exactly . . . would you suggest for plan O, Mr. . . . Oskar?"

Oskar rubbed his hands together. "Well, you're finally coming to your senses, my lad. I was afraid your wife had managed to get all the brains in your family. Anyway, pay attention. We have to get our hands on another vehicle right away. We can't keep toddling around in this bloated carriage, can we? The cops are looking for it."

Tina gulped. "Tell me. Who . . . who exactly are you?"

4

"Oskar Krauss with a double *s*. Rescuer in times of need and, incidentally, the owner of a getaway car."

Tina shot Markus a wary look. *Getaway car* implied things like organized crime, men in black suits, bulletproof glass, and screeching tires. The old man had to be joking. "You . . . you have a getaway car. Where exactly would that be located, if I may ask? At the assisted living in Sonnenberg?"

Markus couldn't hold back a hysterical giggle.

"You won't be laughing for long," Oskar growled. "Or you can just cool your heels in this sickmobile. I'd be glad to show the police the injuries you've given me." He accusingly lifted up a leg, on which a huge dark-blue bruise was forming on the pale skin just above his striped sock.

"Oh!" Tina exclaimed. "That looks awful. But we didn't do that!"

"Tell that to the cops." Oskar pulled his pants leg back down.

"All right, all right!" Markus raised his hands in surrender. "What do you suggest? And where could we find this car?"

"On Amselweg Road. In Ingolstadt. It's only a fifteen-minute drive."

"What?" Markus laughed. "You want us to go back to Ingolstadt? That's ridiculous! We just left. They're looking for us back there. Nothing in the world will make us go back."

"But where should we go instead?" Tina struggled to stay calm and not grab Markus by the collar and shake him. Of course, he had no idea where this idiotic escape was supposed to lead—just like he hadn't thought through *anything* at all.

"I was about to ask the same thing." Oskar shook his head in mild amusement.

"Stop asking so many questions. We'll just drive. I'll think of something." Markus started the ambulance so violently that the siren gave a screech like a mistreated animal. The Aldi bag tipped over, scattering its contents across the floor.

"Watch it!" Annoyed, Tina stuffed the money back into the bag, and then nobody said anything for a while.

Oskar quietly hummed some melody, and Tina stared at the landscape whizzing past them, incapable of gathering her thoughts. They passed two sweating cyclists dressed in extreme sports attire who were obstinately pedaling up the hill. They didn't glance up even once. The trio in the ambulance drove past rapeseed fields and along a lovely chestnut avenue, but they were too occupied with their own thoughts to pay even the slightest attention.

Oskar's humming was now interrupted by a dry cough that the old man fired off with military precision every ten seconds. Rolling his eyes, Markus deliberately fiddled around with the car radio.

Lady Gaga belted through the speakers with the force of a slap. Markus hastily turned down the volume.

"Music today is awful," Oskar remarked from the back, and Tina secretly had to agree with him. What Paul sometimes listened to hardly counted as music. He loved the performers who wore caps on their heads and stomped around onstage like oversize Christmas elves, their pants puddling around their ankles as if they were in the midst of potty training. With huge golden necklaces dangling from their necks, they were tattooed from head to toe with hieroglyphics and strange symbols and sayings in Sanskrit or whatever other language, and were always shouting lyrics that basically said things like: "Fuckyoufuckmefuckyeahfuckfuckfuckbrofuckhofuckyeah!"

"Turn that up," she said to Markus. "They're about to give the traffic report."

"—traffic backed up on the A9. We now have an important announcement. The police are asking for your help. They are searching for an ambulance bearing the number IN-AX 24. After holding up a gas station, a couple stole the vehicle at gunpoint this afternoon after seriously injuring the driver. In addition, they've abducted an eighty-nine-year-old man who was in the rear of the vehicle at the time of the incident. The old man is presumably in grave danger, and the public is strongly urged to share any pertinent information . . ."

Markus switched off the radio. "Crap!" He pounded his fists against the steering wheel and then shot a swift glance back at Oskar. "The driver is seriously injured. They made that up! And 'in grave danger.' I don't see anyone here in grave danger. Do you?" He looked over at Tina.

"Hmm?" Tina hadn't even been listening to him. She had gone numb at the announcement. A couple holding up a gas station . . . What an injustice! Markus had done it all on his own—it had absolutely nothing to do with her! And yet now they were lumped together, as if she were just as guilty. And what if their son Paul had heard that? Then it occurred to her that Paul would never connect such news with his dull parents, whom he assumed to be at their equally dull jobs anyway. Besides, he hardly ever listened to the radio; at the moment, his phone seemed to supply everything he needed in life: a comfort item, provider of music, photo album, information source, and connection with the outside world. Furthermore, Paul wouldn't be home for another two hours.

"Mr. . . . uh, Oskar. Do you need insulin? Dialysis? A pacemaker?" Markus's voice reached her.

"Nope. A beer would be nice, though. And just for the record, I'm eighty-seven. But like I said, that fool of a driver didn't have a clue. Are you sure you didn't hurt him at all? No? That would've been nice. Anyway, I don't need insulin. Does this mean that we can drive straight to Ingolstadt now?"

"I think we should go pick up Oskar's car." Tina looked at her husband. "Or do you have a better idea?"

"What if the cops are waiting for us there, huh?"

"They aren't" was the response from the back. "I never collaborate with the cops. You can bank on that, Marko."

"Markus." He gnawed on his lower lip. "I don't know."

Tina was slowly running out of patience. Markus had gotten them into this hot water, and now he obviously had no idea what to do next except drive around aimlessly like a headless chicken, all because he was too stubborn and vain to accept the old man's suggestion. At the same time, of course, it was a little strange that Oskar was offering to help them in the first place. Why would he even do that?

"Why?" she asked as she turned to face Oskar. "Why do you want to help us? I can't think of any reason for you to do that."

"Finally." Oskar grinned. "Finally we're getting to the gist of the matter. You really should take some remedial lessons in logic from your wife, Marko. And now just listen."

"Markus," Tina corrected.

Oskar scooted his wheelchair toward the front of the ambulance to get closer to the partition wall. "Anyway, listen up, you two hotshots. You caught on that I don't want to go to that lousy nursing home, right? But you haven't asked where I might want to go instead."

"Oh, pardon me. Unfortunately, we've had more pressing things on our minds," Markus interjected, a grim look on his face.

"Forget about it, Marko." Oskar waved it off with a generous gesture.

"Marku—"

"Oskar wants to go home. To Amselweg Road," Tina deduced out loud. It made sense.

"Not exactly. I don't live there. My son-in-law does. He is the biggest moron that has ever set foot on this planet. Useless and lazy, and as greedy as the government. He sits around the house all day, blasting robots to pieces on his computer. I'll never understand what my daughter sees in him. She'd have been better off marrying her refrigerator. It at least brings some food to the table. No, I don't want to go back to my daughter. My son-in-law wouldn't waste a minute to ship me off to the nursing home, and I wouldn't even be able to defend myself since my crutches and my luggage are still at the assisted living home in Sonnenberg. No, I want to go somewhere else." He paused meaningfully. "I want us to get the car in Ingolstadt and then drive up to the coast."

"Me too," Tina exclaimed, both sarcastic and desperate.

"Great! We've got two votes so far. What about you, Marko?"

"Markus. No, I didn't actually plan to drive to the beach today." Markus swerved indecisively between the right and left turn lanes at a completely empty intersection. It annoyed Tina that he was sitting there behind the steering wheel like an irritable monarch in a leisure shirt, when he was actually the cause of all their problems!

"Ingolstadt is to the right, Marko. And I want to go to the seaside. To be exact, to the North Sea. Even more precisely, to Wobbenbüll, near Husum. That's where my house is. It used to belong to my parents, and that's where I grew up, went to school and dance lessons, learned how to swim and later how to drive motorcycles, and my dog is buried beneath an apple tree in the garden. And now my son-in-law thinks he can just get rid of me and sell my home so he can live high on the money. But he's counting his chickens before they've hatched! I want to go home because my home still belongs to me. Who knows how much longer I'll be kicking around down here." Oskar pounded his fist against the armrest on his wheelchair. "And I won't spend my last days dodging around mops and buckets of disinfectant and senile old codgers staring into space. I want to be in my own home. And if I can die there, I'll spend some of my afterlife haunting the old place and scaring off potential buyers, just to annoy my son-in-law." He gave a sharp laugh. "And that's why I want the two of you to take me there. In my car. What do you say to that?"

"We say no to that," Markus replied immediately. "We'll end up stuck in the sticks up on the North Sea, completely broke and with the police on our heels."

"Wobbenbüll isn't the sticks. It's beautiful. And why would you be broke? What about your nice fat haul?" Oskar pointed at the Aldi bag.

"It's only a little over eight hundred," Tina murmured. The holdup at the gas station was all the more shameful in light of the paltry sum they'd actually made off with.

Oskar nodded, as if he had already guessed this. "You know, gas stations. They never were worth the effort, and these days they hardly keep any cash in the registers. Most people don't know that, though. Your plan wasn't the best."

Tina opened her mouth in protest. She was about to say that *she'd* had nothing to do with the plan, and that she and Markus weren't cold-hearted criminals who earned their daily bread through the misfortune of other people, when Oskar quietly continued. "How'd you like to add a few thousand more to that?"

"A few thousand more of what?" Tina squinted as sunbeams flashed through the trees along the edge of the road, momentarily blinding her.

"Euros, my dear. You know, those funny-looking bills we've been using for the past few years that look like pretend money." Oskar winked. "I'm not sure how much they're worth now, but twenty years ago or so, I hid a few things away when it became clear that my daughter planned to marry that moron."

"What . . . what do you mean? *What* did you hide away?" Tina rubbed her temples like she always did when she was stressed.

"My legacy," Oskar declared soberly. "It's actually been earmarked for my daughter since forever, but she and her husband are already getting the house in Wobbenbüll. Before I give them my little treasure up there as well, I'd rather let myself get eaten by sand shrimps. No, I'll split it with you, assuming that you drive me up there, of course. It'll be nice for the money to stay in the family, so to speak. In the Mafia family, right, Marko? *La famiglia?*"

Oskar reached through the open partition window and gave Markus a friendly pat on the back. Under the influence of Oskar's little speech, Markus had turned to the right and was driving toward Ingolstadt as if in a trance. They were now drawing up to one of the first busier roads.

Markus brought the ambulance to a screeching halt at a stoplight, but he still hadn't said anything and was just staring glassily out of the windshield.

"Markus?" Tina nudged him.

Someone next to them honked, and to their horror, they realized that another ambulance had pulled up to the right of them. The stocky driver rolled down his window and waved. "Hi there!"

"Hi," Tina squeaked.

They were done for, now. The other driver would recognize them and call the police. He would wrench them out of the vehicle, probably sedate them with some kind of narcotic, and then strap them down on a gurney. The tabloid photographers would show up then and shoot unflattering pictures of her, and by tomorrow, her coworkers at Fashion World would be talking about it. They would go through her drawers, find her hormone tablets, and congratulate themselves that the obviously crazy Tina Michel was now in police custody, because sooner or later she would've gone after her colleagues with a machete. After all, everyone knew that those on the verge of instability had to snap someday.

"Did you hear?" The driver stuck his head out his window. "They're looking for one of our vehicles. Some criminal couple has kidnapped a patient, some old guy in a wheelchair. And they killed the driver on the spot! Probably in some horrible way. Strangled or something. The Czech mob, no doubt. A man and a woman. Insane!"

Tina tried to sink deeper into her seat without drawing attention to herself.

Shaking his head, the driver continued, "I'm telling you, we're working in a life-threatening field. Life threatening! I risk my neck every day for a pittance. A little while ago, some old guy peed all over the back. And who had to clean that up? Hmm?"

Tina slid down even farther and refused to make eye contact with the other man. Why was it taking so long for the light to turn green, dammit?

"Hopefully they'll catch them soon," the man resumed. "The scum!"

"You're right about that," Oskar unexpectedly interjected, leaning his head through the partition window. "It's hard to believe what kinds of people are running around these days. Anyway, we'll keep an eye out for an ambulance driven around by a couple with an old man in a wheelchair in the back. Be careful out there!"

Tina was practically lying flat in her seat by this point.

"I will be." The man nodded eagerly. "Take care of yourselves too!"

"Of course we will." Oskar waved at the man, and Tina, who could hardly breathe, murmured an indefinite farewell in the other ambulance's general direction.

The light finally turned green, and she swiftly closed the window as they made a left turn. For a fleeting moment, they could see the now-confused face of the other driver in the rearview mirror. He was still sitting at the light, but now he had his phone up to his ear.

"Idiot," Oskar remarked. "Take a right up there, down that little side street," he instructed Markus.

Tina closed her eyes for a second. Any minute, they might have the police on their heels again. Enough was enough. "Just go to Amselweg, Markus. Oskar, we accept your offer." *We don't have any other options,* she thought to herself. His treasure, whatever. But there were also the few thousand euros, whatever the old man had rambled on about. Probably ten thousand pennies squirreled away somewhere. Still, they had to ditch this crummy ambulance. And call Paul and tell him that he didn't need to worry. Or did he?

Markus came to a stop in front of a small park and, with shaking fingers, tried repeatedly to type *Amselweg* into the GPS.

"Don't bother, Marko, I'll tell you how to get there. The back way. You don't want to take any major roads, do you?"

"Markus," Markus replied weakly, before falling silent.

He followed Oskar's instructions. They drove almost soundlessly and at a snail's pace down various peaceful side streets, slinking along the fronts of buildings like a mangy alley cat. Tina recalled a horror film she had watched ages ago, in which some people were abducted in an ambulance. *Spare Parts.* But now they were the kidnappers. How ridiculous. She was just a completely ordinary woman—Tina Michel, forty-five, an employee at an e-commerce company and a mother. She really needed a restroom right about now, and a shower. Her mouth was as dry and dusty as Gandhi's sandals, and her stomach was rumbling.

"We're here," a contented voice declared from the back. Oskar pointed at a plain single-family house. "Our magic carpet is sitting in the garage. All we have to do is get it out, Marko."

5

Tina peered cautiously down the street, which was lined with an array of small barricaded fortresses. A shapeless woman was sitting at the window of the house across the road, her arms spilling across the windowsill like porridge. Her sullen, watchful gaze immediately made Tina feel nervous. This was just the kind of person, a combination of neighborhood watch and gossip, who would call the police with ecstatically trembling fingers, delighted at her ability to defend her tiny realm and to finally have something to do. And even happier because of the opportunity to actually stick it to someone else. Two houses down sat a preschool. Behind the fence, small children staggered around with pails and shovels as a reedy voice piped, "Humpty Dumpty sat on the wall . . ." Two teachers gazed as longingly as zoo animals over the fence into the childless freedom on the other side, where an ambulance had come to a stop, hopefully to bring some action to the boring afternoon.

In Tina's opinion, this wasn't an optimal moment to get out of the vehicle. Everyone around here was bound to know Oskar and his family, and either the nearby neighbors or one of the bevy of parents, all exhausted after their workday and dragging themselves out of their cars to pick up their progeny, would have heard the news.

"Hold on a second," she warned. "The chubby woman over there is watching us closely."

"And what are we going to do about your daughter and son-in-law?" Markus turned to Oskar. "You said that he sits around the house all day, shooting aliens to bits. But he can add two plus two, and then we still won't have a getaway car, but there'll be more trouble and—"

"He shoots robots. And he isn't here." Oskar cut him off. "I know that. Roll down your window and talk to that house dragon hanging out the window over there."

"What should I say to her?" Markus peered up at the facade.

"Ask her to sign a form confirming that we dropped off two old ladies from the Jehovah's Witnesses at her place, since nobody would let us into the assisted living facility."

"What two old ladies?" Markus blinked in confusion, once again missing the point.

Tina leaned across Markus and called out from the window, "Excuse me? Hello, ma'am?"

"Yes?" The woman at the window eagerly puffed herself up.

"Could you maybe help us? We have two old women from the Jehovah's Witnesses with us, and no one over there at the elder care facility would answer the door. Could we drop them off with you? Somebody'll be by to pick them up in a few hours, so all you need to do is sign a form. It'll cover things in case something happens to the ladies in your apartment. It's mostly because of Mrs. Maier. She has a weak bladder. The other one, Mrs. Werner, has Tourette's and flails around from time to time, but is otherwise completely harmless. At least as long as somebody is willing to listen to her talk, which she does nonstop, and—"

"What in the world are you talking about? Get out of here," the woman exclaimed in dismay. "I refuse to sign anything!"

"You would really help us out. We need to hurry. Wait, I'll come out so I can explain everything to you more—"

The woman disappeared, slamming shut the window.

"Bravo!" Oskar clapped his hands. "I knew you had it in you. Marko, though, needs to loosen up a bit."

"Come on, my name is Markus," Markus groaned.

"Now let's go," Oskar exclaimed. "The old bat is gone, and the children are heading back inside. Roll me out."

Tina slipped nimbly out of the ambulance and quickly checked the street. The preschool's activities had been moved to the front of its building, where someone had just shouted "Surprise!" The road was otherwise empty. Markus opened the rear door of the ambulance and unbuckled the strap. Together, he and Tina steered Oskar across the street. All of this happened so quickly and professionally that Tina felt for a moment like she was part of a small, elite, practically aristocratic gang of crooks. The only things that didn't really fit with this image were Markus's striped shirt and his ill-fitting glasses. And the fact that she was rocking side to side because she desperately needed a bathroom.

"The key's under the turtle," Oskar declared, pointing at a small stone turtle sitting in the front yard. "The golden one goes to the garage, and the silver one is for the house."

Tina grabbed the keys, checked their surroundings one more time, and unlocked the garage. She slipped inside, followed by Markus, who was pushing Oskar in front of him. The interior smelled very musty, and when Tina switched on the light, she was met with a desolate scene. In the middle of the garage loomed a VW van, like a white elephant surrounded by a jungle of empty beer bottles, trash, and cables. The garage walls were almost completely covered with heavy metal posters and Playmates of the Month.

"You've got to be kidding me!" Tina couldn't help exclaiming. "And your daughter's okay with all this?"

"Yeah, like I said, Volker is an idiot. See if the keys are in the ignition."

Markus nodded and opened the driver's door. "Yep. They're here. Should I drive it out?"

"Just a sec." Tina couldn't wait any longer. "I really have to use the restroom. Oskar, do you think I could run up and . . . ?"

"Sure! Welcome to the weak-bladder club! Every sneeze a squeeze, right?" Oskar cackled. "Just don't steal the good silver up there!"

His laughter followed Tina up the dark staircase until she reached the living quarters. The house smelled awful. On top of that, Tina had never seen so many photos and posters of naked women in one place before. Women lolling across motorcycles, race cars, construction cranes, and all sorts of other vehicles. Oskar's daughter had to be either blind or dim-witted to let all this go on.

Tina opened a door and found herself in a trash-filled living room in which the smell of cigarette smoke and old pizza remnants engulfed her. The typical nudie pictures and two still lifes—a deer with grapes and grapes with flowers—hung on the walls. Dirt-brown drapes, gray mesh curtains, and a tattered couch the color of nicotine-yellowed fingernails. Oskar's son-in-law obviously had the decorating talent of a nearsighted gorilla. The coffee table held an array of ashtrays and a strangely shaped object, which upon closer examination turned out to be a glass sculpture. A Harley-Davidson made of crystal. Wow. A small inscription was attached to the base. For a moment, Tina forgot about her bladder and leaned down to read the words. Without any warning whatsoever, the figurine tipped over and shattered into a thousand pieces across the floor.

"Shit! Oh, no!" Tina felt herself grow ice cold in shock.

She scurried around the coffee table, crushing the shards of glass even more under her feet, and realized that there was nothing she could do. The crunching of glass screeched in her ear and echoed loudly through the room. What if somebody was at home, after all? She listened, and in the silence somewhere, a telephone rang. She froze in the middle of the room. Who could be calling? The son-in-law himself? Oskar's daughter? The phone rang and rang, and then an answering machine switched on, which was almost stranger than this entire dump of a house. Who still had an answering machine?

"You know what you can't do? You can't reach me. *Beep!*"

The unknown caller obviously decided not to leave a message in response to this charming greeting, and Tina shook off her torpor and hurried off to find the bathroom. She stumbled through a messy bedroom in which an unmade bed functioned as the depressing center point. Oddly enough, it held only one narrow blanket and a single pillow. The couple probably had separate bedrooms. After all Tina had heard and seen of Oskar's son-in-law, she found this completely understandable. However, she didn't see another bed anywhere, though she did find the bathroom. Despite the lack of toilet paper, she sat down in relief, only to discover a few seconds later that the toilet wouldn't flush.

"Dammit!" she cried as she angrily jiggled the handle up and down.

Suddenly water started to fill the bowl but wouldn't flow out. It rose higher and higher and higher, until—to her horror—it started to spill over the edge of the toilet bowl and flood across the floor.

"Markus?" she shouted in panic. "Markus?"

Nobody answered. The two men probably couldn't hear her over the roar of the van engine down in the garage. Tina dashed back down to the basement.

"Markus, I broke the handle on the toilet! There's water running everywhere."

"Marvelous!" Sitting in his wheelchair, Oskar slapped his thighs in delight. "You really are creative, my girl."

"What?" Tina asked in confusion. "How is this marvelous?"

"Well, I'm imagining the look he's going to have on his face." Oskar coughed a little. "My son-in-law, that is."

"But everything's flooding up there!"

"Exactly, exactly." Oskar grinned diabolically.

He was obviously more confused than she'd thought he was. Tina turned toward her husband. "Markus, you have to go upstairs and fix the toilet."

"No way! We're getting out of here right now. I'm not a plumber."

"A plumber!" Oskar howled with laughter, and to Tina's annoyance, Markus joined in.

This day was worsening with each passing minute, and on top of everything else, she had shattered that glass thingy, that dumb motorcycle. Paul had always dreamed of having a Harley. Paul. She needed to call him and tell him . . . what, exactly?

"Come on." Markus tugged on her arm. "Help me get Oskar into the van."

They hauled the old man up into the van, where he immediately made himself comfortable in the back seat. They folded the wheelchair and stashed it in the rear.

"And now let's get out of here." Markus climbed into the driver's seat. "Go out to the street and see if anyone's coming."

"What should we do with the ambulance?" Tina asked.

"Let's park it down the road," Oskar declared. "We don't need it anymore. And this way they won't know it was us who took his car."

Tina hurried out to the street, while Markus followed her and quickly got into the ambulance to drive it away. The only person in sight was a man out walking his dog, and the scent of a freshly baked cake wafted over to her from somewhere. Her stomach clenched. She hadn't had anything to eat or drink since breakfast, and that had only been a slice of toast. Well, there had been a cup of coffee at the Fashion World office, but that had hardly qualified as coffee, more like a hot drink that resembled in appearance and taste the rinse water produced after you had your hair dyed. She should've taken something to eat from Oskar's daughter's house. However, she hadn't really seen anything to eat there. Besides that, she hadn't seen even one photo of Oskar's daughter anywhere. Or anything that indicated that a woman lived there. And no computer. That was strange. Hadn't Oskar told them his son-in-law spent his days gaming online?

Tina didn't have time to give this more thought, though, since she could hear police sirens blaring weakly in the distance. Chattering mothers with balloons were clustering in front of the preschool. *Someone might come down the street at any moment.* Where was Markus? Then she spotted him, sashaying down the street, trying to look as relaxed and inconspicuous as possible. Now he was literally sniffing a rose. She gestured at him frantically to hurry up, and finally, he picked up the pace, slipped behind the wheel of the van, and slowly pulled out onto the road.

Still feeling guilty, Tina closed the garage door behind him and climbed into the passenger seat of the van. She thought she could still hear the water gushing inside the house. "Markus, shouldn't we check the toilet before . . . ?"

"Just forget about the toilet! Do you think Al Capone cared about doing the dishes or fixing clogged toilets after he'd just committed a couple of murders and money-laundering jobs?"

"What are you talking about? Are you Capone now or something?"

"Sorry." Markus lifted his hands apologetically and drove off. "Of course I'm not Al Capone."

"Not yet," Oskar interjected with a snicker from the back. "There's still time for that, don't worry. You don't get to be the top dog overnight. Not like I was ever the top dog, though. Far from it!"

Tina believed him at face value. She couldn't imagine him in a pricey dove-gray suit with a briefcase clutched in his hand. She had no idea what she could envision Oskar doing. A gurgling sound disrupted her train of thought, and a little too late she realized the sound was coming from her own stomach.

"Sorry," she murmured. "I'm starving. I was in the process of getting lunch when my day got completely messed up. Actually—my life. Because someone here totally short-circuited and gave zero thought to what might happen next."

That last comment was for Markus, but he acted as if he didn't hear her as he continued to whistle some melody or the other. Now that he was driving a nondescript van surrounded by rush-hour traffic, he was considerably more relaxed.

"Maybe we could stop and get something to eat," she suggested. "Or is there a chocolate bar or something like that here in the car?"

Why hadn't she at least eaten the peanuts she'd stolen? She opened the glove compartment, and all sorts of papers and empty cigarette packages instantly spilled out. Tina was about to stuff everything back in when her eyes caught sight of something. The registration card for the van, made out in the name of Ralf Kirchmeier.

"Oskar?" she asked slowly. "What's your son-in-law's name?"

"Volker," Oskar replied. "Or Nincompoop, Loser, Bum. Take your pick."

"So who is Ralf Kirchmeier?" Tina held up the registration card and turned to face Oskar.

He avoided her eyes and started to fidget in his seat uncomfortably.

"Oskar?"

"Kirchmeier is an idiot too. An even bigger one than my son-in-law, although he's pretty hard to top."

Tina understood nothing at this point. "Who is Ralf Kirchmeier? Does this van belong to him?"

"Yes. And the house that's getting flooded right now." Oskar started chuckling again at the thought.

"Markus? Pull over right now." Tina poked her husband.

He drove into the parking lot of a small bank and shot a this-isn't-my-fault look at Tina. He turned around toward Oskar. "Who is Ralf Kirchmeier?"

"One of the nurses at Sonnenberg and the biggest asshole on God's green earth. Forgive my language, but there really isn't a better word for him. His favorite hobby is upsetting old people. For example, Mrs. Heidner. She has to talk quietly because she has some problem with her voice box, and he always acts like he can't hear her. Or Mr. Pfalz. He's scared of fish, though I don't know why. There are all kinds of phobias out there, so why not this one? Every day, Kirchmeier maliciously tells him that they're going to move a huge aquarium into Mr. Pfalz's room. And Mr. Pfalz howls and raves and shouts, and Kirchmeier laughs his head off."

"How awful!" Tina exclaimed. "And nobody does anything to stop him?"

"What could they do? Who could do it? No one can prove anything." Oskar wasn't done yet. "And he never gives any of us a bath because he simply doesn't want to. He says three minutes later old people start to stink again anyway."

"He says that to them?" Markus shook his head in disgust.

"Not directly. But on the phone, or to the other nurses. Especially the new ones, so they won't get any dumb ideas about being nice to any of the residents. Besides that, he thinks we're all senile and deaf and suffer from Alzheimer's. He knows no boundaries. And if push comes to shove, he doesn't mind using force." Oskar laughed, albeit somewhat bitterly.

The bruise on Oskar's leg. Tina suddenly understood. "But how do you know where he lives? And where he keeps his garage key?"

"He thinks I'm made out of wood, like Pinocchio or something, and that I don't hear anything. A few days ago, he was talking loudly on his phone to a buddy who was going to spend the night with him. He told him that he always keeps a spare key under the turtle. What an idiot!" Oskar shook his head in amusement.

"And so you . . . ?" For a moment, Tina was at a loss for words.

"And so I did." Oskar winked at her. "I was always something of a Robin Hood. I only stole from the mean, vicious types, never from the good ones."

"And what about your son-in-law?" Markus started the van again and drove back onto the main road. "Does he actually exist?"

"Yes, of course, he does. What about him? He's still an idiot. Wants to put my house by the sea up for sale and to have me declared mentally unfit. Unfortunately, he doesn't have a VW van we could steal."

"I . . ." Tina cut in, but had to stop because she couldn't help laughing. "I . . . I didn't just flood Kirchmeier's bathroom. I also—" She started shaking again with laughter and couldn't seem to stop. It was as if all the stress of the past few hours was being released by a single spasm of laughter. "I also broke his glass sculpture. A Harl . . . Harl—" She took a deep breath. "A glass motorcycle! I just wanted to take a quick look at it, but then it toppled over and shattered into a thousand pieces."

The van swerved a little as Markus almost lost control because he was laughing hard too.

"Gosh, I'm going to pass out," Tina gasped. "When he gets home—"

"—we'll be long gone, on our way to the North Sea." Markus revved the engine.

"I really need something to eat and drink now," Tina insisted.

"I'm hungry too." Oskar looked at his watch. "We always get supper around five thirty, and it's already five."

"We should call Paul," Tina said. At the thought of her son, all of her laughter evaporated. What should she tell Paul? How could she explain everything to him? *Mom and Dad are taking a little vacation without you, and it might take some time for us to get back. We're going on a ten-hour drive with Uncle Oskar, a distant relative, to the North Sea for a few days. True, you've never heard of him. He's pretty stubborn and doesn't like teenagers, which is why you can't come along. Mom and Dad are hunted criminals for holding up a gas station around lunchtime. Oh, and for a bit of kidnapping. Other than that, everything's all right. How was your school day? Supper's in the fridge. Oh, never mind, the fridge is empty.*

She had an idea. "Let's stop by the apartment for a moment. Maybe he's already there, and we can explain everything to him directly. He never answers his phone if one of us calls."

"What if the neighbors see us?" Markus wondered aloud.

"So what? They don't know that we were the ones at the gas station. We got rid of the ambulance. Worst case, they'll think we bought a new car."

"I don't think *new* is the right word," Markus murmured. But to Tina's relief, he turned toward the city limits and headed for their neighborhood.

~

The apartment block looked just the way it had when Tina had left it that morning, assuming that she was facing yet one more torturously dull and uneventful workday. It felt as if a hundred years had passed since that moment, and she fleetingly wondered if she would ever again sit out on her balcony. Would she ever again listen to their neighbors arguing or set up the rusty laundry rack out there?

In the rays of the late-afternoon sun, the building looked downright homey. A few children were playing in the field behind the building, while a couple of teens were lurking near the entrance, smoking. However, Paul wasn't in sight.

"Wait," Tina said as she pulled her phone out and dialed Paul's number.

He didn't answer.

"I'll go up," she said, climbing out of the car. "You two wait here."

"Hurry," Markus called after her. "And bring something to drink. And to eat. And my blue T-shirt."

Tina was no longer listening to him, though; she was too focused on slipping into the apartment building unnoticed. The teens didn't pose a threat of any kind. Tina knew all too well from personal experience that they would register a woman over forty with about as much attention as they'd pay to roadside warning signs or dust bunnies underneath their beds. She stepped into the stairwell and took a deep breath. No one in sight. Encouraged, she hurried up the stairs. Thank goodness they lived on the second floor, which meant there was little risk of her running into any nosy, chatty neighbors.

She took the last two steps in one great stride and suddenly shrank back. A police officer was standing at her apartment door, pressing the doorbell. Tina froze like a deer in headlights, incapable of gathering any clear thoughts. The officer turned toward her.

"Hello," Tina squeaked.

"Do you live here?" the other woman asked. "Are you Mrs. Michel?"

"No," Tina replied automatically. "I'm not. I don't know her. I think I'm in the wrong building." What was she blabbering on about?

At that moment, the door of her neighbor, Mr. Ottwald, opened, and he was suddenly standing right next to them. He was wearing frog-green fitness pants and a World Cup T-shirt, and had two trash bags in hand. Like always, he just stared at her in silence. They hadn't been on speaking terms for a while, not since he had complained about Paul's loud music. At the time, Tina's only defense had been that they didn't even need their own TV since his was loud enough for both apartments. Ottwald had deflected this allegation by questioning Tina's general intelligence level, which then spurred her to describe him as an antisocial meathead who poisoned the entire building with his cigarette smoke. His eyes now slid to the officer and then back to Tina, who shot him a pleading look. *Please don't say anything. I'll never call you an antisocial meathead ever again, I promise. Just hold your tongue and stay as grouchy as always, okay?*

"Uh . . ." Ottwald cleared his throat. "Ms. . . ."

"I'm innocent!" Tina could no longer hold her tongue. "I didn't have anything to do with it. I just wanted to go to get some lunch, I swear!"

The officer gazed at her in astonishment. "Listen, it's obvious to me that you weren't the one who sprayed graffiti all over the basement." She sounded a little annoyed. "But it would make my job a bit easier if I could find someone who could unlock the basement so I can take a look around. Do you have a basement key?" she asked Ottwald.

He cleared his throat again. "Madame Officer, what I was about to say was that somebody keeps letting the air out of my bike tires, down in the courtyard. Has to be mean neighbors." This was obviously aimed at Tina. "That's what the police should be investigating, not some graffiti." He emphasized his request by energetically shaking his trash bags and stomping down the stairs.

The officer watched him go, amazed.

"Men. What can you say?" Tina gave an artificial laugh. She had almost pounded her hands against the railing in relief. They weren't looking for her! Tina wished she could dash off, but how would that look?

Exasperated, the officer pulled her radio out. "Holger, I need someone who can unlock the basement door."

Why wasn't the officer leaving? She stood rooted to the spot in front of the apartment door that Tina couldn't walk through now.

"Well, bye-bye," she said, reaching for the railing. *Bye-bye?* Was she losing her mind?

The officer didn't even glance her way.

"I'll go now," Tina continued as she took a little step backward.

The officer didn't budge but looked up at Tina, her radio still at her ear. "Holger, hurry up," Tina heard her mutter. "And do you think this is some kind of mental facility? There are all sorts of . . . Forget it. Just get up here."

Tina slunk down the staircase like a cat. She heard shuffling footsteps as Ottwald returned from his excursion to the garbage cans. Time to get out of here!

~

"What do you mean you weren't inside the apartment? Where were you the whole time?" Markus stared at her in disbelief.

"There was an officer on the landing, and she was ringing our doorbell. Then Ottwald came out and almost betrayed me, but she wasn't looking for us. She wouldn't leave, though, and I had already said that I wasn't Mrs. Michel. And . . . Just let it go, okay?"

Tina pressed her lips together in anger. Thanks to that dumb officer, she hadn't dared to enter their apartment, and basically that was all Markus's fault. There was so much she wanted to yell at him about, but with Oskar watching, she pulled herself together and just barked "I'm still hungry!" at her husband, who was now driving the van back toward downtown.

"All right, I'll pull over there." Markus pointed at a small kebab shop wedged between a medical supply store and a flower shop. "It's empty, and we can quickly get something to eat while you try to call Paul one more time."

"Yay, kebabs!" Oskar's face lit up. "Finally something other than Bavarian sauerkraut and potato puree."

After parking, they helped him into his wheelchair and stepped into the empty restaurant. The owner barely glanced up, continuing to chat on his phone while they placed their orders. They took their seats in small plastic chairs at a corner table and waited for their food while Tina drained an entire water bottle. Above their heads hung a television, on which a cartoon was flickering. Ending his call, the man behind the counter sliced pieces off the hunk of meat on the spit before laying three flatbreads on the grill. He reached for the remote control to change the station. A news reporter appeared, and Tina suddenly found herself looking at her own photo on the screen. As icing on the cake, it was that awful picture from her passport, the one in which she looked like a drowned corpse. The image switched to a black-and-white video from the gas station's security camera that showed Markus waving his pistol at the cashier. From that camera angle, he looked like a gangster.

"What in the . . . ?" Tina dropped the plastic bottle, and it clattered to the floor.

The phone rang again, and the kebab man resumed his monologue with the other person on the line. Tina and Markus listened with bated breath to the news report and stared at the screen, which now showed Amselweg Road, where a group of gaping neighbors had gathered in front of Ralf Kirchmeier's house.

"The police are still looking for the criminal couple, who have now been identified as Markus and Tina Michel. Today at noon, they held up a gas station, injured an ambulance driver, and kidnapped a care-dependent man, who, according to the Sonnenberg Assisted Living Community, has a life-threatening heart condition. We have just received news that the Michels have been involved with another burglary, this time of a private home owned by one of the nurses at the Sonnenberg assisted living home. The couple likely gained the information needed to access the property by coercing it out of ninety-year-old Oskar K. Our reporter Lutz Koehler is located on site to interview the burglary victim."

A brawny man came into view. He had small, squinty eyes and wore a Metallica T-shirt. Tina assumed this was Ralf Kirchmeier, the nurse and the meanest asshole on God's green earth. How had they found out about them? Markus had parked the ambulance down the road. Had someone in the street recognized them, after all? The woman in the window, maybe?

"They completely destroyed my house and stole my car," the man bemoaned. *"See for yourself!"*

He pointed behind him, and the camera panned across the garage, which still looked exactly the way Tina and Markus had found it that afternoon.

"Here we see an unbelievable scene of vandalism and devastation, dear viewers," intoned the voice of reporter Lutz Koehler, a man sporting both a leather jacket and a microphone. *"And as we have learned here, this is only the beginning. The upper living area is severely flooded because the criminal gang the police suspect is behind all this appears to have deliberately caused a water pipe to burst. They left behind an employee badge from a company called Fashion World, belonging to a Tina Michel."*

Tina looked down at herself in disbelief. Sure enough, that goddamn name badge was gone. She must have lost it when she'd rattled that toilet flush in panic.

"In addition, they wantonly destroyed a valuable trophy belonging to the Harley-Davidson Club of Ernsgaden." The reporter's voice filtered back into her awareness.

The scene switched back to the TV studio, where the news anchor was shaking his head in disbelief.

"It almost feels as if these criminals enjoy tormenting their victims, wouldn't you agree?"

The leather-jacket reporter reappeared on the screen. *"That is absolutely true. We are dealing with an especially cunning gang. By this point, the police experts conjecture that the Michels have lived incognito for many years, and this strike was planned with meticulous precision. A larger organization is behind the whole thing, that much is certain. Eyewitnesses described two older women who were also kidnapped, apparently members of the Jehovah's Witnesses. It is possible that what we have here is some kind of black-market organ-trafficking gang. Of course, we continue to hope that Oskar K. is still alive. Signing off from Ingolstadt, dear viewers."* He nodded morosely, as if he had just reached the end of a eulogy. Up next, a report about an upcoming strike of garbage workers.

"Food's ready," the man behind the counter called out.

"Food's ready," Oskar repeated cheerfully. "Do you mind getting it? It's a little difficult for me, with my wheelchair and everything. Don't forget I'm actually eighty-seven, and not ninety as the dummies on the news keep claiming. Just watch, by tomorrow, I'll be ninety-five and a hundred the day after that. And what'll I be after that? A mummy?"

At that moment, Tina's phone rang. Paul! Finally. She quickly pressed the green button.

"Mom?" she heard him say. "Mom, some cops are here. And . . . what they're saying isn't true, is it? You're still at work, right? Are you coming home soon? Mom?"

6

As Tina listened to Paul's voice, tears sprang to her eyes. What was she doing here? How had her life changed so completely within such a short time? She could be at home right now, putting her feet up, warming up a few noodles from yesterday, watching a little TV, and tousling Paul's hair, despite the fact he always rolled his eyes at her. In short, she could be having a totally normal and boring evening, like all the countless other evenings before now. They suddenly struck her as idyllic and peaceful, all because they were now unattainable. Starting today, nothing would ever be the same.

"Mom?"

"It's Paul," Tina mouthed as she frantically gestured at her husband. "Paulie, dear," she whispered. "It's not what you think. It's—"

"Mom, they want to talk to you. The co . . . the officers."

In the background, Tina could hear various voices talking away. Someone said, "Give that to me," and Paul replied, suddenly sounding quite childlike, "Do I have to answer questions now?"

"Paul?" Tina cried into her phone. "Paulie? Hello?"

Somebody took the phone out of her hand and turned it off. Tina whipped her head around angrily and gazed into Oskar's wrinkled face and eyes, in which a tiny cheerful spark had always been visible. But now, Oskar looked a little worried as well.

"Please forgive me," the old man pleaded. "But you know that they're trying to locate you right now, don't you? The longer you chat with your son, the greater the likelihood that they'll be able to find you. Able to find *us*."

Helplessly, Tina glanced around the kebab shop as if she hoped to gain some kind of insight from the business owner. With his phone now clamped between his chin and his shoulder, he was listening to someone as he sliced away on a new piece of meat. "But I have to talk to Paul. He's our son. Who knows what he's going through! Markus, say something. This is all your fault, after all!"

At this moment, she felt furious at Markus. It *was* his fault. Never in her life would it have occurred to her to hold up a gas station. This was the kind of stuff that only men dreamed up. Nearsighted, testosterone-fueled, impulsive, stupid men, who, when faced with stressful situations, could only tap into a few parts of their limited primate brains. Well, maybe that went for desperate men too. As Markus just sat there, staring at his kebab, he looked completely spent.

Exhausted, he nudged his flatbread back and forth on his plate. "Yes, it's my fault. And I'm so terribly sorry things have gone this way, Tina. Honestly. If you like, I'll publicly admit that I acted alone and turn myself in to the police, and you can . . . you can . . ."

"She can visit you in jail?" Oskar shook his head as he carefully wiped his hands on the paper napkin, which he then balled up and dropped onto his plate. "I think we're done wallowing in self-pity now. Nobody's going to turn themselves in. The cops would throw themselves the biggest party ever if they got their hands on some idiot who willingly walked into their precinct. They'd pin ten other things on you from their unsolved case files. Just calm down." At this, he gave Tina's arm a pat. "The best thing right now is for both of you to throw away your phones." He started to toss Tina's phone in a high arc toward an overflowing trash can full of flatbread pieces and cabbage, but Markus was able to block the throw at the last second.

"Not the entire phone, Oskar. Just the SIM card. The phones were pretty expensive." He pulled the SIM cards from both his and Tina's phones and threw them away.

Oskar rolled the two steps to the trash can and discarded the rest of his meal and napkin as well. "Sure, sure, expensive, you say. And for some totally unnecessary doodad at that. People go into debt to buy these expensive things, and then spend the rest of their lives staring at them and trying to figure out how to pay off what they owe."

Tina fiddled with her now completely useless phone in her lap and finally stuffed it into her purse. How were they going to contact Paul? She suddenly didn't feel hungry anymore, and on top of that, the kebab seller now kept glancing over at them. Had he heard the news on the TV as well?

"We need to go," she urged. "They're bound to be looking for the VW van as well now. What should we do? We have to get away from here as fast as we can! Take the train?"

"Absolutely not. I'd like to actually reach the North Sea before I turn ninety. No, we just need to find another vehicle," Oskar casually declared.

"You mean, we should steal another one?" Tina's voice rang shrilly through the room, and the kebab seller looked up and walked over to their table.

"Everything okay?" he asked. "Food tasty?" He pointed at Tina's full plate. "The meat is really fresh."

"Of course," Tina hurried to say. "I've just lost my appetite. I'm afraid we have to go and . . . pick up our son, you know."

Two men entered the restaurant and also stared at them. Tina ducked her head, grabbed the terrible Aldi bag with all the cash, and stood up.

"Come along, Grandpa. Grandma's waiting for you," she said loudly and pushed Oskar toward the door.

~

"We could kidnap Paul," Tina suggested as soon as she, Oskar, and Markus were sitting once more in the van. "I mean, that's not actually what it would be. He's our son, after all. Parents kidnap their kids all the time."

"And how would you go about that?" Markus asked. "Put on a disguise, ring the doorbell, and yell *Good evening, everyone,* before grabbing him by his backpack? It sounds like the police are already there."

"How old is your Paul?" Oskar interjected.

"He just turned eighteen."

"Marvelous!" Oskar's face lit up. "In that case, they can't do anything to him. He'll finally have the apartment all to himself and can have his girlfriend over."

"Paul doesn't have a girlfriend yet," Markus protested with dignity. He started the car and lowered his window. "He's never mentioned a girl. Although to be fair, he never mentions anything to me anyway."

Oskar chuckled loud and long. From outdoors, the sound of young people laughing floated toward them, like an echo, from the street corner where some teenagers were standing.

"What? Did I say something funny?" Markus hissed at Tina.

"I think Oskar is implying that Paul definitely has a girlfriend." Tina couldn't help smiling. "Her name happens to be Amelie."

"But how—" Markus started to bluster, but Tina interrupted him.

"That doesn't matter right now. We have to find a way to contact him. And we desperately need a new car. And where are we going to spend the night? We won't make it up to the North Sea, at least not today. I can't drive for nine hours straight. Oskar can't drive at all, and Tina . . ." He fell silent.

Tina hadn't driven in decades—not since that thing with Susi happened and . . . No, she didn't want to think about that now. And she certainly wasn't about to start again while on the run.

~

They agreed to cover a few more miles yet that evening and to stop in some town along the way. From there, they could try to call Paul from a public telephone, "arrange" for a new vehicle under the cover of darkness (the thought of which made Tina feel queasy), and then register for a room at some small hotel as an ordinary couple accompanied by their disabled grandpa. Somewhere where the crickets chirped and the internet didn't really work all that great.

They drove for a while along a country road, then a highway, and Markus turned the radio on. An oldies station. Dire Straits was soon belting out "So Far Away," followed by Bruce Springsteen singing about his "Hungry Heart." A sleepy calm spread through the car. Oskar nodded off, the warm sun beamed down through the cloudless sky, and each time they passed an RV, Tina felt almost as if she were on vacation. This was utterly ridiculous, of course, since they were on the lam. It had been ages since they had gone anywhere, not even spontaneously, and definitely not to the beach. She had met Markus twenty-five years ago while on a camping trip along the North Sea, but they hadn't been back since then. Why not? Tina stole a glance at him from the side as he stared tensely at the lane, and she spontaneously patted his leg.

"Hey," Tina said. "The North Sea. Do you remember?"

"Of course I remember. You were wearing purple pants and some kind of triangle earring. And . . . what was her name again, your friend? You two kept struggling to set up your silly tent."

"Susi." Tina grinned. "She works for the police now and has been through two divorces."

"That's it, Susi. Well, hopefully she's learned how to set up a tent by now. I can't tell you how much I wanted her to just disappear for a while. There was no way to get to you. Susi was always right next to you, all buttoned up, and she kept discouraging you from doing one thing or the other. A total killjoy. Why were you friends with someone so uptight?"

"She wasn't really all that uptight," Tina said before she could stop herself.

She bit her tongue as soon as she said that. She had promised Susi back then that she wouldn't tell anyone about the agreement the two of them had made. And Tina was a woman who kept her word, even if the entire matter was over and done with, and she was only occasionally in touch with Susi. It was three years since they had last chatted, and that was only because they had run into each other at the hardware store.

"What do you mean?" Markus asked, confused.

He switched lanes to pass an RV from the Netherlands, which had enough bikes attached to the back to service a large family.

"Oh, nothing. You eventually found a way to talk to me anyway," said Tina, evading the question.

She suddenly envisioned Markus the way he had looked back then—hair down to his shoulders and a guitar strapped to his body, and faded jeans to boot. He had made one wisecrack after the other, and at the end of two days, it was clear to her that she definitely wanted to see him again after that vacation. There was something so easygoing about him; he took each day as it came with little concern for the future. At the time, she had found this extremely charming and admirable. Twenty-five years later, however, the admiration had faded significantly, and Tina was mostly annoyed by his spontaneity. Markus had never kept any job for long, spinning grander and grander plans that never came to anything. And even the best of relationships could end up going down the tubes in the face of chronic money shortages. All you had to do was look at the situation he had gotten her into today. Tina sighed. Nonetheless, looking back, those had been the best weeks of her life. In the evenings, they had sat around the campfire, drinking red wine as Markus played his guitar and Tina tried in vain to hook Susi up with Matze, Markus's buddy. Matze eventually informed her in a whispered tone that he wasn't into granny types, and Susi overheard and spent the rest of the vacation feeling insulted.

Where was the guitar these days? Paul had never shown any interest in learning how to play, or in music in general. Tina now recalled that at some point Markus had stuck the instrument up in the attic. The guitar—symbolic for their own youth—now rested among boxes stuffed with old clothes that no longer fit and diaries brimming with ideas and dreams that nobody cared about anymore, in a dark space that no one ever entered. Except perhaps to extract the Christmas tree stand once a year.

Neil Young crooned from the speakers about wanting to live. Markus rumbled along with him, and Tina joined in—too deep and flat, but so what.

"You really need to practice a bit more," Oskar quipped from the back seat. "You two aren't quite the Carpenters yet."

"Thank goodness," Markus replied.

He let a BMW cut in front of them so it could catch the rapidly approaching exit.

"I'd rather be Sonny and Cher," Tina declared.

"Oh? You know them?" Oskar seemed surprised.

"Of course. They were popular long before our time, but we still rocked out to Cher, didn't we, Markus?"

"Maybe you did, but I was never a fan of old Cher. Among my friends, listening to pop music was a form of social suicide."

"She isn't all that old. Late sixties, right?"

"Seventy-nine," Oskar shot back.

"Wow. She looks really good, in that case." Tina wondered briefly what she would look like at seventy-nine but realized that she didn't really want to know.

"Everything all nipped and tucked and put back together again." Markus waved this off. "A human puzzle. Like all the other famous folks. The women look alike these days, like pussycats but blond."

Tina started to laugh, then stopped abruptly. "How do you happen to know that, Oskar? Cher's age, that is."

"I met her once."

"What?" In his surprise, Markus almost rear-ended a Polish semi chugging along in front of them. "You met Cher? How? When?"

"In the sixties. It must've been 1966, I think. After she'd hit the big time. Sonny was still with her."

"Where did you meet them? At a concert? Did you get their autographs?"

"No. I photographed them."

"How?" Tina thought she'd misheard him.

"With a camera, my dear. Not with a phone like you all use these days. If someone had told me back then that fifty years down the road, people would be constantly shooting pictures with their phones, I would've thought they were crazy. What is it?" he asked Tina, who was staring at him, her mouth open. "Back then, our phones were as large as soccer balls. If I'd had to drag something like that around with me—"

"I didn't mean *how* did you take the photographs," Tina interrupted him. "I meant how did you end up doing that? How does a retiree from Ingolstadt manage to photograph Sonny and Cher?"

"I wasn't a retiree back then, thank you very much. And secondly, I'm from the North Sea, like I already told you. I just landed here because . . . well, it's a long story. I was a photographer and actually did a lot of shoots . . . That's what I did before . . . well, anyway."

"Before you got started as Robin Hood?" Tina asked slowly. "You said something about that as we were leaving Kirchmeier's house, didn't you? What did you actually mean by that? And who were the *nasty guys* you took stuff from? And what did you take?"

Oskar mumbled something.

"Cars, maybe?" she probed further, when Oskar remained doggedly silent.

"Among other things. Cars, motorcycles, later TVs too. I took a boat once. Sometimes a little coke and hash. Cash. This and that."

Tina was astonished that Oskar simply admitted all this. "You were a criminal?"

"Criminal?" Oskar asked back. "Well, I think it's always a question of perspective. I was, first and foremost, a gentleman."

"He *was* a criminal," Markus chimed in. "We count as that now, too, Tina."

There was no response to this. Speechless, Tina watched the landscape whizz by from her window. Out there, fields; in here, criminals.

"Anyway, Sonny was a slimeball," Oskar said. "In case that interests you two. Oh, the exit for Nuremberg is coming up. We should take it."

"I thought we wanted to get to the North Sea." Markus started to slow down.

"Of course, but it occurred to me that Magda lives in Nuremberg. An old friend of mine. We could stay at her place tonight. Maybe she even has a car we could use."

Tina hesitated momentarily, but the prospect of ditching Nurse Kirchmeier's dumb VW van was extremely tempting. Besides that, she was past ready to sit down quietly somewhere and stop rushing around and looking over her shoulder. She wanted to consider what all had come down on her today. They hadn't had a single moment to collect their wits. And she wished to call Paul.

"Does Magda have a landline?" she asked.

"Well, I seriously hope she still does," Oskar replied. "It used to ring off the hook, back in the day." He laughed a little oddly.

What did he mean? It didn't matter. In a large city like Nuremberg, you stood out less than you did in a small town. That much was sure. And there would be plenty of cars sitting around, waiting to get stolen. A moment later, Tina felt terribly ashamed. How could she even think something like that? And in fact, neither she nor Markus had ever stolen a car before. What had become of her life?

"Okay, let's go to Nuremberg, Tina. I really want to get out of this van." Markus switched lanes, took the exit, and drove past several hardware and furniture stores as they headed into the city. "We're almost out of gas too."

Tina grasped the situation immediately. They were going to have to take *this* VW van to a gas station. The second gas station of the day, with security cameras and all that. Never!

"I should call Magda right away," Oskar said. "Pull over at that bar over there. They'll have a phone."

They parked in front of the Golden Tankard, a nondescript suburban pub whose dingy white facade blended seamlessly into the dismal commercial neighborhood.

~

Acting nonchalant, Markus rapped on the bar and vanished in the direction of the restrooms, while Tina, nervous, her heart pounding, ordered a soft drink as a way to justify her presence.

"A soft drink," the barkeeper repeated, studying her scornfully. "And Grandpa here?" He turned toward Oskar. "A cup of chamomile tea?" He smirked slightly.

"Nope. Keep that for yourself," Oskar replied in disgust. "I'll take a beer. And I'd also like to make a local call, if possible."

"The phone's over there," the man growled, though Oskar's order seemed to placate him a little.

Tina nervously watched as Oskar rolled over to the counter where the phone was sitting. Besides the three of them, the only people in the bar were two silent men who were sitting at a corner table and staring straight at them. Tina averted her face. What was keeping Markus so long?

"Magda, old girl!" she heard Oskar crow enthusiastically from the counter. "How are you these days?"

Thank goodness this Magda was at home, at least. Tina sipped on her soft drink and glanced quickly to her left, where the two men still sat over their beers without talking. Instantly, one of them looked back at her; he seemed equipped with some sort of built-in radar. Was there so little variety around here that he had to stare at her so hard? Finally, Markus returned from the restroom.

"Well, you know, as we get older, beauty creeps inside us." Oskar's voice boomed from where he was sitting at the counter. "Ha ha! Huh? Just say it!" He drained half of his beer in one gulp.

Tina drummed her fingers impatiently on the table. Now one of the starers got to his feet and walked past them. Then he came to a stop and looked back at her. "Say, do we know each other from somewhere?" he asked.

Tina froze, dread twisting in her gut. Her likeness was guaranteed to be flickering on every screen in the country at the moment. The fact that this man had recognized her from her drowned-corpse photo was also profoundly depressing.

"No, I don't think so," Markus answered on her behalf, before helping her to stand up. "Osk—Grandpa? Are you done yet?"

"Liquid Viagra, you don't say?" Oskar continued to chatter away without a care in the world. "And it'll be administered to the elderly intravenously? Hahaha! Magda, you do beat the band!"

"Grandpa!" Tina called out, her voice shrill.

"You're Sabine Kunz, aren't you?" the man now said to her. "You used to live around the corner from here!"

"No," Tina rasped. "I'm not her. I'm . . . Mrs. Krauss." Why had she said that? She was obviously out of her mind. "Kraus with a double *s*," she added lamely, as if that made any difference at all. The man peered at her, a shadow of doubt darkening his face.

Oskar finally hung up, rolled his chair back a little, and accidentally knocked his beer glass over on the counter. "Oh, goodness!" he cried. "I'm really sorry about that."

The barkeeper rolled his eyes. "It's all good, Grandpa." Then he mumbled something to himself. It sounded like "Chamomile tea would've been better."

"No, no, just wait, I'll wipe it up," Oskar declared eagerly. He reached across the counter and started to fumble around.

"Grandpa, we have to go now," Tina hissed, but Oskar, oddly obstinate, kept wiping and fiddling around with the counter until she literally dragged him away.

They hurried outside with the wheelchair, while the two beer drinkers and the barkeeper stood gesticulating at the window, their excitement palpable.

"I think they recognized us," Tina whispered as she tried to somehow cover the stupid Aldi bag with her arm. The clinking of the coins inside it sounded very loud to her.

They stowed Oskar along with his wheelchair in the back of the vehicle, and then Markus started the engine and sped out of the parking lot on squealing tires. "Now where to?" he asked, his voice tight with tension. "Where does Magda live?"

"Stay cool," Oskar said. "Let me count my money first. Just keep driving along this road."

"Do you have her address?" Tina wanted to know. "Otherwise, Markus won't know . . . Wait, what money?"

"The money from the barkeep back there," Oskar explained. "Chamomile tea . . . He's the one losing it."

"You stole his money?" Tina looked at the old man, aghast.

"The till was open, so about half of what was there. I could've taken more if you hadn't dragged me away, my dear. Chumps like him don't deserve better."

This topped everything. "Honestly, I can't believe it. Markus, are you listening? Have you lost your mind, Oskar? They'll send the police after us!"

"The police are already looking for us," Oskar pointed out matter-of-factly. "A little extra cash won't make any difference. Four hundred thirty euros. Not bad, if I do say so myself. Here, add this to the kitty." He handed Tina the money and pointed at the Aldi bag sitting at her feet. "To get to Magda's, turn right at the next stoplight. Then straight on to Altenfurt, where she lives next to the post office. Can't miss it. You'll like each other."

"We will?" Tina stared out of the window.

~

Magda was a 28 DD, wore her artificial titian-red hair piled up into an airy updo, had wide smiling lips from which a cigarette dangled, and was somewhere between sixty and eighty. She was clad in a peachy velvet suit.

"Oskar!" she cried with delight. "You're still alive and kicking, you old monster. I can't believe it! And you look awful, like an old prune on wheels!" She pressed Oskar against her ample chest. "And who did you bring along? Your family? Your daughter and her husband?" She studied Tina and Markus curiously and shook their hands.

"No, these are . . . business partners. Do you remember the chubby guy who always wore those dumb-looking striped suits and wanted to be a sales rep for a greeting card company?"

"Yeah. Did he die, or is he in jail?"

"Much worse. He married my daughter."

"Oh no! And there was nothing you could do about it?"

"Nothing, Magda, absolutely nothing." Downcast, Oskar ran his hand over his bald head.

"Ah, you have to tell me all about it, but first, come inside. How about a cocktail?"

"Not for—" Tina didn't get any farther than that before Oskar poked her in the back. "That would be lovely."

Oh God, what had they gotten themselves into? Tina looked around. Magda's apartment looked like an interior designer's nightmare. Every square inch was covered with straw flowers, carved wood figurines, throw pillows bearing cute sayings, velvet drapes, lamps with pom-poms, and fake fruit. Photos of Magda as a young woman, blond and even more voluptuous than now, hung everywhere on the walls. A few of them showed her with several other young women, all of whom looked rather alike.

"Man, Oskar, the girls will be over the moon when I tell them you came for a visit," Magda chattered away. "They're scattered all over the world now."

Ah, Magda must have daughters. Well, at least that's something, Tina thought. You could always find stuff to chat about and share when it came to kids.

"Are these your daughters?" she asked in interest, tapping one of the photos. "We have a son, Paul, who just turned eighteen."

"Daughters?" Magda chuckled. "No, my dear. I don't have any kids. I was just talking about my call girls."

7

The cocktail was bloodred and saccharine sweet, and represented a kind of appetizer, because it was followed by pink prosecco, which Magda graciously called *bubbly* and even more graciously poured out. Tina fidgeted back and forth in her plush armchair, not quite certain about what she should say except "Thank you, but I don't really want . . . oh okay, a little bit more . . . uh, not so much . . ."

Then she gave up and let Magda top her off as she studied the pink curtains with their flowering tendrils, which were swaying gently in the wind. Or perhaps it was just the alcohol that was making them wave back and forth in front of her eyes. She listened to Magda and Oskar's reminiscences, while Markus smoked one cigarette after the other. Officially speaking, he had given up smoking a year ago, but all the rules and restrictions seemed to have been suspended today. Tina no longer actually cared if he smoked or danced a jig on top of the table or swung from the chandelier. She was just happy about their little breather.

"And Elke, you know the one with red hair who everyone in the club called Coco, she moved to Bulgaria and opened a beach bar there. And no, I don't know why she picked Bulgaria. I bet a man was behind it. And Gerlinde, we called her Magic Mimi, now runs a flower shop in Cologne. And Rosita married one of her johns. Do you remember that thin little guy who was so timid and who always carried a briefcase around with him? As it turned out, he was super rich. Who'd have thought it? He was as stingy as Scrooge. He eventually married Rosita so he didn't have to keep paying for her. And then he died six months later, and she got it all." Magda enthusiastically slapped her thighs, and her breasts shook like they were in a mid-level earthquake.

Oskar pursed his lips in amazement. "Rosita was always entrepreneurial," he remarked. "I assume she helped things along a little."

"You bet she did!"

Shocked, Tina nudged Markus hard in the ribs with her elbow. They were talking about murder!

"She screwed him to death," Magda declared flatly, probably noticing Tina's horror. "He had heart problems and wasn't supposed to get excited. But never in a million years could he have shared a bed with Rosita every night and not gotten excited!" Magda and Oskar roared with laughter, and then Magda gave everyone refills on the bubbly, disregarding Tina's weak protest.

"I thought she might've smothered him with her ample bosoms," Oskar remarked, which set Magda off into peals of laughter again. Markus even joined in this time.

"It is so nice of you to let us stay the night," Tina remarked. "Hopefully it's not an inconvenience. We'll be gone before dawn, so we can take Oskar to Husum. After that, we'll . . ." She cleared her throat, not knowing how to continue.

She actually had no idea what they would do after that. She'd managed to throttle any thoughts along that vein. It all depended on the next move by the police and if they could reach Paul again. "Could I perhaps use your telephone?"

"Of course!" Magda pointed at her wall phone.

She refilled all their glasses as Tina dialed their home number.

The receiver was picked up immediately. An unknown man's voice echoed through Magda's living room; she had obviously set her phone permanently on the speaker setting. "Hello? Michel household."

Tina froze. She didn't recognize the voice. Who was that? An officer? Where was Paul? What should she do now? She sent Markus a pleading look, who, in the process of lighting his next cigarette, went rigid. "Who is that?" she mouthed, holding her hand across the phone.

"Hang up!" Markus gestured so wildly that his glasses slipped down his nose again, but Tina couldn't move.

"Hello?" the voice asked. "Who's there?"

"Is Paul . . . ?" Tina rasped out, before falling silent.

"Mrs. Michel? Is that you?"

At that moment, Magda stood up and took the receiver out of Tina's hand. "Am I speaking with Paul Michel?" she trilled. "This is Andrea Letzow from Paper Mac, Incorporated, the leading manufacturer of printer paper. You've bought paper from us several times before. At the moment, we're having a sale on our products, and we wanted to inform you about this personally. We know you're interested in saving money on your next paper purchase, right?" Magda winked at Tina. The voice on the other end of the line was silent for a moment.

"He isn't available at the moment, and please don't call back. You're blocking the line." The phone went dead.

"The cops are just as clueless as always," Magda commented with quiet pleasure.

"But how are we supposed to contact Paul now?" Tina was on the point of tears. The situation was completely hopeless.

"Email?" Markus suggested.

"He never checks it."

"What does he check?" Oskar inquired.

"How would I know? Instagram, something like that?"

Magda nodded. "Then we'll just use Instagram."

"I don't follow him on Instagram," Tina murmured. "He won't let us. His profile is private . . . Paul's embarrassed by us." She sighed. "I could send him a text, but I don't have my SIM card anymore."

"Wait a sec. I'll do it." Magda pulled a phone in a golden case out of her pocket. "What's his number?"

"But if a Magda . . . What is your last name?"

"Kowalski. Magda Kowalski," Oskar answered for her.

"Thank you. If a Magda Kowalski writes him, he definitely won't respond. I know that much. *I have* to be the one to write him. And what happens if the police check his messages? I have no idea what we should do." Tina dropped down onto Magda's soft couch.

Magda rolled her eyes. "You must think I just fell off the turnip truck. Until last year, I ran a sex chat and text service. A bit of a side hustle, you know. What's the name of his school? I need some point of reference."

"Ebert High School," Tina replied, perplexed. "Why?"

"Okay." Magda started to type, and remarkably fast for a woman her age, at that. "Done." She held her phone out for Tina and Markus to see.

Hi handsome, I go to Ebert too. WYD

"What does WYD mean?" Markus asked.

"What are you doing?" Magda interpreted.

"You can be as old as Methuselah and still learn something new." Oskar had pulled off his shoes and propped up his wool sock–clad feet comfortably on Magda's couch. "Ahh. It is so nice to be back in a room that doesn't just smell like old folks."

"I'm still young and luscious," Magda replied with a smile. She continued typing without looking up. "Just turned seventy-five. Look! He's answered." She held the phone out to Tina. Who is this? 😉

"Okay," Magda said. "What should I tell him?"

"That Mom and Dad aren't criminals and that we love him," Tina offered.

"No," Markus objected. "That we screwed up, and he should hold the fort until we can get him."

"Okay, then what?" Magda typed out I'm trouble and added a winky emoji.

You cute or what? Paul wrote back.

Magda giggled. "Your child isn't a shy one, is he?"

Tina tried to concentrate on what type of message she could send to Paul that would both inform and reassure him. But how was she supposed to do that while her son, her baby, was swapping flirty texts with a luscious seventy-five-year-old madam?

"Markus, we can't tell him that or he'll get scared." Hold the fort until they could get him . . . Good grief, they weren't in a war. What would Paul think?

"Spicy, winky emoji again." Magda tapped away at the phone before lighting a cigarette.

"What?" Tina watched her, stunned.

"And here comes the eggplant!" Magda giggled. "Now we definitely have his attention."

Tina flinched and exchanged a horrified look with Markus. "Paul probably doesn't even know what it means," she hurried to say.

Magda just grinned. "Okay, decide quickly. What should I tell him?"

"Okay." Markus stood up and paced the room like a contemplative philosopher. "Tell him that things went badly today, that we'll be back in touch soon, and . . ." He paused for a moment. "That we hope he's doing all right."

"Okay." Magda typed and then held up her phone.

☺ hak from Ps. today was low key ohio. phone ftl. ttyl asap. w8 there. cwyl. 143

"What in the world is all that?" Tina didn't understand anything except *Ohio* and *phone*.

"Hugs and kisses from parents. Today was stupid. Phone is gone. Talk to you as soon as possible. Wait there. Chat with you later. I love you."

Paul's response was immediate. np gucci x

"No problem, all good. Kisses." Magda gazed cheerfully at Tina and Markus. "And that's that. Bubbly? Cocktail? Cigars?"

"Wow, that was almost creepy." Markus dropped back onto the couch like a sack of potatoes and rubbed his eyes. "I'll take some more."

"I'm going to freshen up a little." Tina stood up.

Her head was spinning, but either way, Paul had sent them a kiss. That was something new.

She stumbled through Magda's plushy den, a kind of purgatory for Japanese minimalists. She passed by epigrams (*Having the biggest paintbrush doesn't make you the best painter* and *Enjoy life to the fullest / You'll be dead longer than alive*), as well as porcelain angels, crocheted afghans, and empty golden bird cages. The bathroom was done up in pink, a sweet scent wafted from several small bowls of dried rose potpourri, and the extra toilet paper roll was stuck in a cream crocheted dress. Curious, Tina opened the medicine cabinet. Toothache relief, painkillers, medicine bottles, arthritis salve, mouthwash, toothpaste, hair spray, makeup samples from the drug store. She instantly felt ashamed that she was spying on Magda. What had she expected? Handcuffs and lubricant? The woman was in her mid-seventies! Nonetheless, Tina wondered what things must have been like for Magda and her . . . girls. Had Oskar been one of their regulars? Everything Tina knew about escort services came from tabloids, mostly in the form of screaming headlines, such as Raid on Hotbed of Vice! And from crime shows in which some balding, leather jacket–wearing detective stormed into a dim establishment with soft rock playing in the background, knocking over glasses and waving his gun around while an ambitious young dancer peeled her clothes off behind him.

Years ago, she and Markus and a few friends had gone to Amsterdam, where they had strolled through the red-light district. Tina recalled the suggestively dressed women sitting in display windows like sales merchandise. They had knitted and chatted while the tourists, grinning stupidly, staggered past them. But she couldn't see how any of that fitted in with Magda.

In the hallway, she studied the photos once more. This time, she noticed a man who showed up in quite a few of the photos alongside a much younger and thinner Magda. Her pimp, perhaps? Where was the guy now? Had she "helped him along" a little too?

Back in the living room, she found Oskar about to light a cigar. Markus had nodded off on the couch. This wasn't all that surprising considering that he usually fell asleep at home in front of the television.

"Magda is fixing up your room," Oskar informed her.

"Thank you." Tina sat down. "Who is the man in the photos out in the hall? Magda's pimp?"

"That's Ludwig. Her husband. He died a long time ago."

"Oh. Did she . . . ?"

Oskar stared at her indignantly. "Of course not. Ludwig was the love of her life. He's been gone over forty years. Died suddenly from a heart attack. That's why she had to quickly come up with some way to earn money. Magda goes to the cemetery every day and talks to him. She still misses him so much." Wrapped in his own thoughts, he stroked one of Magda's soft pillows.

"She never got remarried?"

"No. She never even dated another man. The two of them fit like two old slippers. You only find something like that once in a lifetime."

Awkward. Tina fidgeted in her chair. She and her dumb prejudices. Why shouldn't someone like Magda be able to find true love? And for that matter, for such a long time, even beyond death. Incredible, really. She watched Markus, who was now snoring softly with his mouth open. Did she even still love him? Right now she almost hated him because he had screwed up their lives with his act of sheer stupidity. And now he had the audacity to fall asleep like a baby instead of worrying. Instead of finding a way out of this misery! Because he was clueless, never thinking things through. But even before today, between their ongoing fights about money, their chaotic daily lives, and their few vacation days, they never had time for each other. And if she were honest, she had imagined more than once what it would be like to meet another man. She almost envied Magda, who just then returned to the room.

"I was telling Tina about your Ludwig," Oskar said.

Magda's face instantly softened, and nothing of the glib madam remained. "My Ludwig. He was the best man in the world." She nodded toward the sleeping Markus. "Be glad you still have him, my dear."

Tina gulped. Glad? Was she? She woke Markus up and guided her sleepy husband into Magda's guest room, where she dropped wearily onto the bed and closed her eyes. When she opened them again briefly, she flinched in surprise, but then she had to smile.

"I can't believe it, Markus," she said. "Look up at the ceiling. There's a huge mirror hanging over the bed." She giggled.

But the only sound Markus was making was even snoring. Tina turned on her side and also fell asleep. However, right before she drifted off, she wondered about Oskar's wife. He hadn't mentioned her even once, but he had a daughter, so there had to be a mother somewhere. Strange.

8

"Oskar, you can't be serious!" Markus was walking around the car that was sitting in Magda's shed like some forgotten time machine. "You can't be serious," he repeated, this time with unconcealed panic in his voice.

Tina didn't say anything. She just held the awful Aldi bag with its ridiculous contents limply at her side. She was exhausted. After a few hours of deep sleep, she had entered a tangled dream in which she tried desperately to take the order from *Mr.* Scheller but couldn't understand him because somewhere in the background a police siren was screeching the entire time. Mr. Scheller had grown increasingly angry on the phone, while from somewhere Magda had kept calling, "But it's out of stock, my dear!" Completely rattled, Tina had woken up and caught sight of her reflection floating above her. In that waking moment, she was convinced that she had been in a car accident and was lying in a coma, while her bodiless soul floated above her hospital bed. But then everything had flooded back to her—the gas station, the stickup, Oskar, Ralf Kirchmeier's house, and Magda. After that, Tina had tried in vain to fall back asleep, because the most incredible thoughts were galloping wildly through her head like runaway horses. She had spent the rest of the night lying in bed wide awake and worrying. By her side, Markus had gurgled, whistled, sawed logs, gasped for breath, and even giggled in his sleep once. At that, she had irately whacked him on the head with her pillow. What right did he have to laugh in his dream while she was too worried to even sleep?

This was why she was now too tired to get upset about the car in Magda's garage, despite the fact it looked absolutely dreadful. A Volvo 850, almost thirty years old, in pink with black silhouettes of go-go girls printed on it along with the words TUTTI-FRUTTI—THE HOTTEST YOUNG FRUITS IN THE CITY!

"I can't drive around in that." Markus shook his head in horror.

"Of course you can," Oskar countered. "My wheelchair will fit in the back perfectly, and the phone number on the side doesn't work anymore anyway."

"But . . . I'll feel like . . ." Markus felt Magda's eyes on him and swallowed the rest of his commentary. "We don't want to attract any attention," he added halfheartedly.

Oskar brushed his concern aside with a sweeping gesture. "We won't. What's the big deal? Look, the license plate is from Hamburg, to boot, from when Magda was living up there. But she doesn't drive it anymore and has graciously offered it to us. And there's no way the police will be looking for us in something like this."

Tina was a little less confident about that fact, but what other options did they have? The VW van would be concealed in Magda's shed, where nobody would be able to find it. "Thank you, Magda," she said as she subtly jabbed Markus in the side. "We'll make sure you get the car back somehow, once we reach our destination."

Which was what? a little voice inside her head mocked her.

"Don't worry about it." Magda gave a magnanimous wave. "I don't need the old girl anymore. Now get out of here. It's starting to get light outside."

She stood there in front of her house, freezing in a salmon-colored housecoat. The first rosy glimmer was spreading across the horizon, and it was almost 4:30 a.m. If they could make good time, they should reach Elysium on the North Sea by late afternoon, or wherever it was that Oskar wanted to go.

"Thank you, Magda," Tina said again, and then she impulsively gave the surprised older woman a quick hug. "For the car and the bed for the night and . . . everything." Magda gave her a wink, hugged Tina back, and then helped Oskar into the car. They stowed the wheelchair in the trunk and drove off, this time with Tina in the back seat so that Oskar could be more comfortable.

The car smelled a little odd, simultaneously sweet and musty. There was a suspicious stain on the back-seat upholstery, which Tina avoided touching. As they set off, a strange clattering came from somewhere in the car's depths.

"Man, Magda, she's a firecracker, isn't she?" Oskar remarked with a shake of his head.

"You said it." Markus came to a stop at a light, where a group of pedestrians was waiting to cross.

Dead-drunk pedestrians, as it turned out. A group of young men, who had obviously been celebrating a bachelor party and were emerging at dawn from some nightclub. The future groom was wearing a baseball cap bearing the words TRAPPED FOR LIFE, as well as an apron announcing I COULD'VE HAD THEM ALL, BUT I JUST WANT MELANIE. He was holding a cornucopia-shaped mug out of which beer sloshed. The others were wearing black T-shirts with yellow print (TOBY'S BACHELOR PARTY), in addition to braided blond wigs and Tyrolean hats. They were all in varying stages of pre–alcohol poisoning.

Suddenly, one of the men with bloodshot eyes stared at the pink Volvo and laboriously deciphered the ad across the doors. A blissful smile spread across his face.

"Toby!" he shouted, taking a few wobbly dance steps toward the car. "A brothel on wheels! How cool is that?"

The others immediately turned to look, and a few seconds later, Tina found herself surrounded by intoxicated men who were pounding on her window, staring inside, and saying stupid stuff.

"Is that one of the hot fruits back there?"

"Old man, what are her rates?"

"A little older than a young fruit, aren't you?"

Tina's cheeks burned with shame. Markus honked like crazy, but the mob of young men wouldn't move aside. Quite the opposite—the groom began trying to climb up the hood of the car. He lost his cornucopia, while one of the guys in braids licked the outside of the back window and grinned at Tina. A couple of the others called, "Take it off! Take it off!"

"Floor it," Tina hissed at Markus.

"How? I can't just run over them."

Thanks to all the honking, a few nearby residents opened their windows, and one voice shouted, "Be quiet, dammit!"

That was the moment Tina caught sight of the patrol car that was leisurely gliding across the street a short distance ahead of them. It would be only a matter of seconds before the uproar attracted it in their direction.

"Markus, just go. The cops are up there!" Tina cried. Why didn't he just drive off? The light had turned green a while ago.

Oskar opened the glove compartment and pulled something out. In a moment of panic, Tina thought he'd grabbed a pistol, but it was only a bundle of black flyers printed in pink letters. Oskar opened the window a crack and shoved them out to the wild mob. "We're just the marketing crew, guys," he explained, easy and relaxed. "But with these flyers, you can all get a free round . . . You know how it works." He grinned. "Summer special at the club."

The men eagerly jerked the sheets out of his hand, and the groom rolled down off the car, which allowed Markus to finally hit the gas and roar off. The last thing Tina heard was a furious shout, "Man, these shitty flyers are for a club in Hamburg from twenty years ago!"

Oskar closed his window. "Melanie's really won the lottery with that Toby, hasn't she?"

With resounding laughter, the three of them sped out of Nuremberg.

~

Oskar suggested that they avoid the autobahn by taking the B8, which would allow them to easily drive down side roads through little villages, if needed. They had almost reached Würzburg when the strange clattering in the car turned into a disturbing rumble. Tina glanced out the window and noticed billows of white smoke coming out the back of the car. "Markus, you have to stop!"

Markus drove off to the right and struggled for a few moments with the whining engine before it gave one last gasp and died with a quiet cough. "Dammit all," Markus cursed under his breath. "Don't worry, we'll be up and running in no time."

He climbed out of the car, walked around to the front, opened the hood, and stared down at the engine for a while. With a grim look on his face, he then walked behind the car and stared for a while at the exhaust pipe. He finally sat back down behind the wheel. "Crappy car."

"Hey, you can't look a gift horse in the mouth," Oskar reminded him.

"That may be. But there's a chance you might have to look in a gift car's cylinder head if it breaks on you."

It was all Greek to Tina. "Is that bad? Cylinder head?" She wasn't quite sure what that was.

"Yes, it's bad. It's why the engine isn't working." For some mysterious reason, Markus seemed to know what was going on. He had some real hidden talents, it seemed.

"Can you fix it?"

He sighed. "No, unfortunately not."

"We could call the roadside assistance—" Tina broke off. How dumb of her. "Sorry. I forgot we let that membership go."

"We did," Markus confirmed, sounding tired. "We're no longer members anywhere at all. We're—"

"You're members in my club." Oskar tapped his chest cheerfully. "And in my club, a broken-down car is nothing to cry about." He pointed out the window at a yellow sign, which announced BIEBELRIED 1 KM. "We can walk that far. There's bound to be a new car in Biebelried, if you know what I mean. It's still early enough for one to get to work."

"Sure, one can get to work," Markus groaned. "But who exactly do you mean by *one*?"

"Me."

"Okay," Markus agreed instantly. "Then let's get cracking. I literally have no idea what we should do next."

Tina opened her mouth to protest, simply because Markus had given in so quickly and this bothered her. But then she had to admit to herself that she didn't have a better solution either. Except to search for a bus stop—but then what?

~

The walk along the road to Biebelried felt a little like a peaceful pilgrimage, even if it was only half a mile long. Markus pushed Oskar along in his wheelchair, while Tina walked behind them, cursing the fact that she had decided to wear pumps to work yesterday. Why had she done that? Nobody ever dropped by the Fashion World office; she and Marion and all their coworkers sat there in their gray cubicles like lab rats, taking stupid orders or letting themselves be bawled out over the telephone by customers mad that one thing or the other hadn't been delivered to them. The clothes the employees wore didn't matter in the slightest. It would've been just fine if they showed up at work in their pajamas or a clown costume or wrapped in a thermal blanket. How in the world had she ended up with this pointless job in the first place? At what point had her life slipped so far off the rails that she'd agreed to spend her days trapped inside a gray box made of particle-board walls, where she had to let herself be yelled at in exchange for minimum wage? And she was supposed to feel grateful for this opportunity! When she was young, Tina had always dreamed of a career as a fashion designer. But that meant going to college—ideally in London or Paris—and there was no money for that. Instead, after school, she spent her days standing alone in a boutique, rehanging expensive clothes for arrogant customers. That's why the job at Fashion World had seemed like a lucky break:

something in fashion, regular hours, nice colleagues . . . The utterly hopeless monotony of the job, however, had sucked any kind of energy and joy out of her.

~

Inhaling the fresh morning air, Tina marveled at the sun, which was now hanging round and plump in the sky. She let her eyes wander across the fields of wheat. Somewhere, a cuckoo was calling, and not even one car passed by. What a beautiful morning! The world was so peaceful at this time of day. She was normally unaware of this since she spent every morning rushing to catch the streetcar, her thoughts rattling through the list of things she needed to take care of after work. Annoyed by the heat, annoyed by everything. And as she realized that, regardless of how all this turned out, she would never return to Fashion World, a feeling of elation flooded through her. She was as free as a bird! A hunted woman, but free, nonetheless. At least for the moment. Marvelous. She should enjoy this day and not rush around so much. And give Marion a call when she could.

"Know what, you two?" she called out to the others. "We should have a nice breakfast somewhere. A really nice one, I mean. Not just a quick muffin and coffee in a paper cup. We have the whole wad with us, after all." She gave the Aldi bag an energetic swing.

"Excellent idea!" Oskar agreed cheerfully. "The muffins at the Sonnenberg home were always day-olds. And let's not talk about the disgusting oatmeal. Oatmeal . . . as if we were all just old farm horses who wanted nothing but oats. Nope, I want scrambled eggs and lox and horseradish and Swiss cheese and crusty bread."

~

The restaurant La Boulangerie had already opened its patio for breakfast guests. A scrumptious scent of coffee and pastries hung in the air.

Servers in black aprons flitted between the customers, who were enjoying the view of the nearby park. The café was so upscale that the lush bouquets on the tables were real, the silverware was heavy, and the coffee was strong.

"Oh, this is so nice!" Tina leaned back in her chair and relaxed with her stomach full of croissants and fresh fruit.

"And did you hear how they tortured him! Just awful!" These words rang out from a nearby table, where two older women in nautical leisure wear were eating breakfast. "He has a heart condition, and they probably refused to give him his medicine. It was in the newspaper. The cannibals!"

"You mean *savages*," the other woman replied. "The poor old man. So awful! You just can't think about what all could happen to you these days." She took a hungry bite from a roll covered thickly with honey.

Alarmed, Tina listened closely.

"I always carry pepper spray with me," the first woman declared. "And if they want to try to kidnap me, they'll get a face full of that!"

"Who would want to kidnap you?" the second woman asked, her mouth full.

"Oh, who knows? They might want my organs. They say there's a lot of money for those on the black market."

"Well, those folks always travel in pairs. You won't get far with your pepper spray. A man and a woman. I heard the woman is a real monster."

Tina swiftly undid her braid and combed her hair into her face with her fingers. She pricked Markus's hand lightly with her fork. Markus was already eating his second refill from the buffet, and his eyes were glassy with happiness. He wasn't registering anything else at the moment.

"Hopefully, they'll catch them soon," continued the conversation from the adjacent table, "so they can free that poor old man."

"Oh, he's probably dead already, you know. They buried him in the woods somewhere."

"Check, please!" Tina whispered to the server who was just passing them. Luckily, he heard her and returned with an elegant flourish.

"Keep the change." Flushing deeply, Tina pulled out several bills, quite a few too many, and the server immediately grew overly solicitous.

"That's why you just have to stay grateful to still be alive, right?" To Tina's dismay, Oskar had inserted himself into the conversation at the neighboring table. "And to have loving children to take care of you and not stick you in a retirement home."

"You're so right!" the woman with the roll crowed enthusiastically. "And to have someone who will still take you out to such a nice café." She smiled at Markus, who stopped chewing long enough to look confused.

"Come on, let's go!" Tina hissed.

"Well, I hope you enjoy your meal," Oskar continued, unperturbed. "We have to get moving now. Have a lovely day!"

"Likewise," the two women replied in unison before resuming their conversation.

Tina pushed Oskar's wheelchair so quickly that she was soon out of breath. Up and around the corner and down a side street with a downcast Markus in tow, who was still bemoaning his abandoned breakfast. On the side street, they found themselves beside a little church with a shady graveyard surrounded by a small wall. Tina came to a stop, breathing heavily. Suddenly, a grinding sound could be heard from below. She glanced down to see where the sound was coming from.

"What the . . . ?" Oskar's wheelchair lurched to one side, and as if in slow motion, the large wheel on the back right came off the chair. Tina barely managed to grab on to Oskar, otherwise he would have landed on the pavement. "I can't believe it. I really just can't believe it! What a crummy wheelchair!"

"I'm a public health patient. What else could you expect?" Oskar stared at the broken wheel. "But as I see it, God has had mercy on us. He has led us straight to a church—and what do my eagle eyes see over there?" He pointed up ahead. Indeed, in front of the church stood a car.

Nothing special, nothing conspicuous, just an older silver VW. "Perfect for our needs. The gray mouse among the cars. Old enough to not have any complicated security features, but if I'm not mistaken, with a window that is open just a crack." Oskar struggled to his feet out of the slanting wheelchair and shuffled slowly over to the car. There, he braced himself against the car and glanced quickly around. He then pushed his right hand deftly through the crack. "I almost have it," he said to Tina and Markus, who were watching him, mesmerized.

"Can I be of assistance to you?" A man's head suddenly appeared over the top of the small church wall. He was wearing a gray blazer over a black shirt with a collar on which a small white rectangle glowed. The pastor! Tina went rigid.

"Oh, I'm only leaning here for a moment." Oskar didn't bat an eye. "My wheelchair just broke. I didn't want to sprawl out in front of your church. How would that look? As if my loved ones had abandoned their gravely ill old father in front of a house of God, right? Ha ha! We aren't living in Luther's time anymore, are we?" He discreetly withdrew his hand from the window.

The pastor didn't say a word but studied the three of them thoughtfully. At that moment, Tina was certain that he had been watching them and knew exactly what Oskar had been about to do.

Crap. She took a breath. The dream was over now. Wasn't it?

The pastor cleared his throat.

9

What the pastor said next was the last thing Tina expected.

"Wait a minute. I have a wheelchair over in the congregational building." He nodded toward the white building directly adjacent to the church. "If you'd like, you may borrow it. Until you get a new one, that is."

"That would be amazingly helpful," Tina blurted out. How were you supposed to address a pastor like this? "Your Reverence," she added a little feebly.

The pastor's lips twitched in amusement. "Pastor Georg Schroeder will suffice. Most people just call me Georg. Do you live nearby? I don't recall seeing you around here before."

"We're tourists, so to speak . . . Just heading through." Markus avoided making eye contact with the pastor as he said this. He was scratching away at the crumbling church wall with marked interest, as if he were trying to extract a stone sample as a souvenir.

"Heading through," the pastor repeated. "Ah. Where are you going?"

"We're going to—" Markus began.

Tina gave him a nudge. "Our car broke down too," she hastily interjected before Markus could say anything else stupid. Things were starting to get a little uncomfortable. Maybe they should just turn down the offered wheelchair and carry Oskar around. But how? Piggyback, like when they were kids? Back in junior high, they'd had to do that in PE, but that was over thirty years ago. Tina could still remember how she'd been told to carry around her classmate Sabina Walter, and how she'd almost collapsed after a couple of steps, and how the other girl had breathed heavily down her neck and clung to her like a gorilla. Tina had practically choked on the mingled curse of teenage sweat and body odor.

Oskar interrupted the rather embarrassed pause. "My wheelchair and our car were obviously manufactured by the same company. And I'll tell you a secret—it wasn't Mercedes."

To Tina's relief, the pastor seemed amused. "In that case, follow me." He turned toward Oskar. "Can you manage? It's just up there."

"No problem." Oskar gave a jaunty wave, but Tina could tell that walking was difficult for him.

They crept along toward the congregational hall. Markus reached for Oskar's arm and discreetly supported him. Tina shot her husband a thankful look. It was finally dawning on her what a completely crackpot idea this entire endeavor actually was. Oskar could hardly walk, and if they hadn't run into the nice pastor, their trip would've ended on the steps of this church, which was probably how things were about to go anyway. They wouldn't be able to purchase a new wheelchair or a new car with the few bills they had taken from the gas station. And obviously it wasn't turning out to be all that easy to "acquire" one of these in some other way.

"Are you really okay? If not, I have a pair of crutches in the car. I tore a ligament a few months ago." The pastor came to a stop and pointed back at the silver VW.

Tina's cheeks flushed darkly. They had almost stolen the pastor's own car! In a few seconds, they'd be struck by God's wrath; a slate shingle would plunge through their heads. Or a fist-size piece from a comet or the discharged waste from a leaky airplane.

Once they reached the congregational building, they gently set Oskar down on the small bench next to the entrance. Ivy was climbing all over the facade, and a brass door knocker was evocative of times long past. A display case mounted next to the door provided information about upcoming events. Pastor Georg unlocked the door, fetched the newspaper from the mailbox, and deposited it carelessly on a carved chest of drawers right beside the door. He then set off in search of the wheelchair. "It's probably parked against the rear wall of the parish hall," he called over his shoulder.

"Thanks again!" Tina shouted back. Her glance then fell on the newspaper. Criminal Couple Michel have obviously disappeared. No trace of Oskar K. Is he even still alive? Underneath this headline, her awful photo stared back at her once more. In the grainy black-and-white newspaper image, Tina looked like a cross between Snow White's evil queen and a homeless drunk corpse. A photo of Markus from his driver's license was included next to hers; his smile looked diabolical, somehow. The newspaper had also dug up a picture of Oskar, which showed him in the midst of a group of senior citizens. They were facing an Advent wreath and a few coffee cups. The majority of those in the photograph were grinning in a way that suggested they were always grinning like that, whether the table in front of them held an Advent wreath, the foreign minister of Japan, or Taylor Swift. Two of the older people were dozing with their mouths open, while Oskar himself had his arms folded across his chest and just looked angry.

"Markus!" Alarmed, Tina held the newspaper out to her husband.

He gasped for air. "Shit!"

"Here it is," the voice of Pastor Georg rang out. Something clattered as footsteps drew closer. He was coming back.

Thinking quickly, Markus reached for the newspaper and folded it such that the back side of the newspaper with the weather report was facing up. He set it down on the chest the very second Georg rounded the corner with the wheelchair.

"Well, it isn't new anymore, but it will do the trick. Better than nothing."

"Ah, that's a snappy new number compared to my old clunker." Oskar stood up and sat down in it right away, inadvertently knocking the newspaper off the chest. The paper sailed onto the floor, slyly spreading out and revealing Tina's awful photo once more.

"What do we owe you for the use of the wheelchair?" Tina asked, her voice tight. She shot a meaningful look at Markus, who bent down to tie his shoelace and surreptitiously refold the newspaper.

"Not a thing. It's all good. Just drop it off when you come back this way."

That was exactly the problem. There was no coming back, not even the slightest notion of coming back. Good Lord, there wasn't even the slightest notion of getting away, beyond making it to that silly Wobbenbüll.

"It might be some time before we come back through here. What would a wheelchair like this cost?" Tina rummaged around in the Aldi bag.

Something fluttered past her leg. To her dismay, bills were slipping out of the bag, which clearly now had a hole in it. In next to no time, a small mound of money had piled up at Tina's feet, as if she were some kind of money conjurer.

Georg looked at the mound and then at Tina, and once again, she could have sworn that he knew more than he indicated. This stupid Aldi bag. They must have mentioned it in the news reports. How dumb could she really be?

"My daughter has a credit card phobia and hates banks of all kinds." Oskar deftly switched gears. "She always hauls all her cash around with her. Quirky habit, I know, but she gets it from me. I've never trusted the banks. Do you know why they never have public bathrooms?" He leaned forward confidentially. "Because no one wants to deal with the deposits." Oskar broke into cackles of laughter, while Pastor Georg chuckled in vague confusion. Tina twisted her bag into a rope, and Markus slipped a comforting arm around her.

"Ah, a credit card phobia. My aunt used to have aulophobia, a fear of flutes. Whenever she heard Mozart's flute concerto, she would start to tremble. I could never understand that. How could anyone be so scared of flutes, which have never done anything to anyone?" If the pastor thought that Tina suffered from a mental disability and urgently needed therapy, he didn't indicate that. "We'll find some way to get the wheelchair back. Have you had breakfast already?" he chatted on. "Would you like to have some coffee with me?"

"Well, we should have time for a cup of coffee, right . . . Grandpa? I mean, Dad," Markus floundered. "What do you think, sweetheart?"

Tina swallowed. She thought it would be impolite to turn down the invitation. "Sure, why not?"

"Wonderful! Follow me. And don't forget your money. Oh, would you mind bringing the paper along too?"

Markus exchanged a dismayed look with Tina, then reached reluctantly for the newspaper, as if it were a dead rat. Tina leaned down and began stuffing the money into her small purse. Only half of the bills would fit, so she made the impulsive decision to shove the rest of the money into a wooden box sitting on top of the chest of drawers. Wasn't that the offering box? Oh well. The pastor could use the money to buy a pair of new bull's-eye window panes, or new altar paraments, or an especially melodic bell. She was simply done with this stupid money. This . . . blood money. Had the pastor recognized her earlier? What if he asked to see the newspaper?

"Coming!" she called out to Georg, who was already pushing Oskar into the kitchen.

"Markus, what should we do now?" she whispered. "He looked at us so strangely. He suspects something. Maybe he's already notified the police."

"When?" Markus whispered back. "We were with him the whole time. Don't worry. It'll be all right."

"Will it?"

"Cream and sugar?" Georg asked from the kitchen.

"Just milk for me, please," Markus called back. "And black for T—for my wife." He brushed a strand of hair from her face. "I swear to you that I'll find a solution. This time, I really will. Let's take Oskar up to the North Sea first, though. And maybe there really is something to what he said about his money."

Tina frowned. "You don't actually believe that. Oskar is clever. How else could he have convinced us to drive him up there? Just be real for a second."

~

The newspaper lay on the kitchen table like a bomb that could go off at any second. Georg didn't look at it as he busied himself with coffee filters and cream pitchers, showing no signs of concern. But it was only a matter of time until he discovered the photos. Markus took Oskar to the restroom, and Tina found herself alone with the pastor. She set her money-stuffed handbag on top of the newspaper.

"Where are you actually heading?" Georg asked, without turning around.

"Oh, we're spontaneous about things like this. Or rather, my husband is spontaneous," Tina murmured. "We're heading north—for a while, anyway."

"It doesn't sound like you necessarily want to go that way." The pastor still didn't turn around.

"I'm doing this for my husband's sake. Coming along on this trip north, that is. Sometimes he acts childish, but he doesn't mean anything by it, and then he really screws things up . . . figuratively speaking, that is. This is why I have to come along. We belong together, after all." She realized that this really was the truth. They belonged together, and she couldn't just leave him in a lurch. "That's the way it is when you love somebody." What in the world was she saying? Because the pastor wasn't facing her, it felt like everything swirling inside her was just coming out now. She hadn't come here for confession or anything. She should just hold her tongue. She was blabbering her way deeper into a whirlpool of inconsistencies. And what could a pastor like this even understand about love?

Georg set a couple of cups down on the table. Tina picked one up and studied the delicate pattern on it. "Pretty design," she remarked in an attempt to change the subject.

"What kind of health problems does your father have?"

"My father? It's been a few years since he di—" Shocked at herself, Tina dropped the cup she was holding, and it plummeted onto the kitchen's stone floor and shattered into a thousand pieces. "Oh, crap! I mean, I'm so sorry!" The pastor's questions had flustered her. "I hope that wasn't an heirloom piece."

"IKEA," he replied with a grin.

Tina exhaled. "I meant that my father's disabled, has been for a few years. It was kind of a stupid accident, but since then, he's been wheelchair bound." This couldn't get any worse. She stood up. "I should go wash my hands. I'll leave my purse here, if that's okay." She pointed at her bag, which was blocking the newspaper, thanks to its bulging girth. If she was lucky, the pastor wouldn't try to push it aside.

"Of course, that's just fine. Nothing gets stolen here."

Nothing gets stolen here. Was that some kind of veiled warning? A hint, maybe? She was slowly growing paranoid.

In the hallway, she discovered Oskar leaning against a bookcase. He was just slipping something into his pants pocket.

"Oskar!" she hissed in horror. "You can't steal anything from here. Absolutely not!"

"Of course not. How can you even think that of me? I already told you that I only steal from idiots. I'm just looking at his books."

"Then what did you just stick in your pocket?"

"A tissue. My nose is running. You don't want me to drip all over the car later on, do you?"

"We don't have a car anymore," Tina reminded him in a hushed voice.

"We'll manage something. Don't worry." He grinned and held a book out to Tina. "Look at this." It showed the silhouette of a man wearing a hat with blood dripping from his hands. "The good reverend likes to read thrillers."

"Really?" Tina pulled another book at random from the bookcase. *The Most Beautiful Love Poems of All Time.*

"Not just thrillers." She opened the book. On the first page, someone had written a dedication.

There once were two royal children,
who loved each other so dear.
They could never be together,
too deep was the water clear.

For my Georg, always
My love, C.

Tina hastily closed the book and glanced around. They'd be done for if the pastor caught them going through his private possessions, especially after they'd tried to break into his car, stuffed their ill-gotten money in his offering box, and broken his china. This was none of their business, and they had to get out of here as fast as possible. Markus emerged from the restroom and agreed with her.

"Come on, Oskar," he said. "We need to get going. Maybe we can still reach Shangri-La by tonight."

"Wobbenbüll," Oskar corrected him.

"I know, I know. Just wanted to make sure you were really listening."

"Marko, I'm starting to like you!" Oskar stumbled a little as he swung his arm to punch Markus in the shoulder, and Tina caught him. She held the old man for a moment and struggled against an impulse to squeeze him tightly, like she would her own father. What would they have done without Oskar, she wondered. Would they still be racing around in the ambulance like a bunch of panicked chickens? Or would they have gotten caught a long time ago? Somewhere deep inside, she knew the depressing answer.

She heard someone clear his throat behind her, and turned around. Pastor Georg was standing at the doorway, watching the almost tranquil tableau they had created—a bookish couple on a journey, the wife affectionately hugging her sickly old father.

"I just wondered how you were planning to resume your trip?" Georg asked. "Is your car at a shop?"

"No," Tina replied, as her cheeks reddened. "It was beyond repair. I think. Right?" She glanced at the two men, seeking their support.

"We'll probably take the train." Markus fiddled with his hands.

Oskar nodded in agreement. "You know how traveling by train is these days—full of surprises. And people. Ha ha!"

Markus laughed along with him, albeit a little too loudly. "Exactly. And that way you can see more of the landscape and get to your destination all relaxed. Assuming you actually manage to get there. Ha ha! Anyway, where is the station from here?"

"Station?" Pastor Georg shook his head, amused. "It won't help you. There's a railroad strike today. Can't you tell?" He nodded toward the window, as if to draw their attention to the silence outside as a result of the missing trains.

"Well, then." Markus shrugged. "We'll have to take the bus."

"The bus workers are also on strike. The entire regional transportation system is at a standstill. I guess the unions think they'll achieve more by working together."

"Well, then," Markus rasped out again, this time with noticeably less enthusiasm. "Well."

In Tina's opinion, it would be for the best if he just stopped talking now. Then they could leave, and then they—that is, Oskar—could get around to "organizing" a new car, and . . .

"If you want, you can borrow the congregational van to drive to Würzburg," the pastor suddenly suggested. "Your options for continuing on your way will be better there. All you'd need to do is park the van in front of Parish Hall South, where my fellow pastor will pick it up.

Just drop the keys off for him in the church mailbox. I was supposed to take the van up there today anyway."

Tina stared at him in disbelief. Did he honestly mean that? Or was he about to break into hoarse laughter as he jerked open the door and made a secret hand gesture to the SWAT team lurking behind the hedge with its black-clad sharpshooter escort? She could tell that Markus and Oskar were just as bewildered as she was. Oskar had even lost his normally glib tongue.

"Really?" she couldn't help asking.

"Why not? I assume you aren't criminals, right?" Georg laughed amiably at this mental image.

Tina, Markus, and Oskar laughed along hysterically.

"No," Oskar replied as he wiped the tears from the corners of his eyes. "We truly aren't. Right, my child?" He smiled at Tina.

"Great! Then it's all settled. You can leave the wheelchair there, too, but only if you've managed to find a replacement by then. I'll call my colleague and tell him that you'll be heading his way shortly. It's only a fifteen-minute drive, after all. They need the van for a youth group event this afternoon."

"Youth group, how nice." Tina's voice sounded as if somebody had taken a cheese grater to her windpipe. She still couldn't believe their good fortune, and as if on autopilot, she reached for the car keys the pastor was holding out to her.

"All right, then—Godspeed!" he said, as he handed something else to her. Her purse.

Tina felt her cheeks flush, because in his other hand he was holding the cursed newspaper. He waved it at them. "And now I'll put my feet up for a moment and see what's going on in the world. Although most of the time there's nothing but BS in here. You can't believe even half of what they print."

"You're telling me," Markus stammered.

"Ah, what a shame it's raining," Georg observed as he opened the front door. "Has it been raining in Ingolstadt too?"

"No, it's been blazing hot," Tina replied automatically.

She instantly bit her tongue. Oskar gave a warning cough, and Markus squeezed her hand tightly. They hadn't mentioned anything about coming from Ingolstadt!

The pastor looked her straight in the eye. "Well, have a good trip. And the best of luck to you! I hope everything works out for your father."

With that, he gave a quick wink.

10

The summertime landscape whipped past the window—fields, meadows, power poles. The sky was a dazzling blue, and over their heads circled a flock of birds. Crows, perhaps? Some kind of black bird that Tina was incapable of identifying. She had long held the opinion that large birds were, for some reason, malevolent and frightening, with their shifty eyes, bony claws, and hoarse caws that always reminded her of the angry tirades of frustrated old people.

The short rain was over, and the remaining puddles on the country road steamed in the morning sun. A few cows were dozing in a meadow, but Tina hardly registered them. Why had Georg helped them? He definitely knew who they were; there was no doubt about that. The seal of the confessional was real, but none of them had confessed anything. Besides, Tina wasn't sure if Georg was Catholic or Lutheran; she couldn't tell the difference. Her experience with church was limited to a childhood Nativity pageant, in which she had spent an hour sweating onstage in a donkey costume. In her bulky gear and to the horror of the entire pageant audience, she had somehow crushed the manger holding the plastic baby Jesus doll.

Anyway, they would never know Georg's actual motivation, but when she thought of the book inscription, Tina remembered something.

"Oskar?" She gripped the folded wheelchair she had stowed next to her seat. "What happened to your wife? I mean, the mother of your daughter." Perhaps they hadn't even been married to each other. "Is she still . . . I mean . . ." She faltered.

Oskar, who had made himself comfortable in the front seat, looked at her in the rearview mirror. "You don't need to sound so solemn. We aren't in a graveyard, my dear. And the good Erika is still very much alive, since you want to know. She's probably shooing her husband through a supermarket, shopping list in hand. Bad weeds grow tall, and Erika is the stinging nettle queen of all the weeds in this world."

"Her husband?" Markus pushed his glasses up his nose again.

"Her second one. We got divorced over thirty years ago. Just a second . . . that makes it over ten thousand days without Erika. That in and of itself is cause to celebrate, but I assume the pastor doesn't have any little liquor bottles stashed in his van." Oskar opened the glove compartment and rummaged around in it. "Nope, too bad. Just cough drops."

Bewildered, Tina didn't say a word.

"We were only married for a few years," Oskar explained. "And that was only because Erika got pregnant. I couldn't just leave her high and dry. She was much younger than me. She was an attractive woman, I must admit, but her voice even back then was about as seductive as a dental drill, especially when she had something to nag about, which was often the case." He broke into a wide grin. "And in the long term, our marriage wasn't sustainable. That was obvious. After that, I tried to remain in contact with my daughter over the years, but we never really warmed up to each other. By now, she's a lot like her mother—never content, greedy, and always a little cantankerous. Ever since she married that moron, the two of them act like they should've gotten their hands on her inheritance the day before yesterday. He wanted to have me declared mentally incompetent ages ago. But he forgot something!" Oskar tapped a finger against his head. "As long as the control center up here still functions, he won't be successful." Oskar sighed. "I never should've married Erika back then, but hindsight is always twenty-twenty. And besides—" He broke off.

"Besides what?" Tina leaned forward in interest.

"Besides, my heart always belonged to someone else, but I couldn't have her. It's just the way it was. Life is like that sometimes."

"And why couldn't you have her? The other woman, I mean?" It appeared that Markus was also getting curious. He wiggled in his seat and pulled in his stomach for a moment. The seat belt was apparently too tight.

"Ah, it doesn't matter. Everything was such a long time ago. And as for Elise—there's no telling where she is these days."

"Elise?" Tina prodded. Now she really was interested. Why did she have to drag everything out of him?

"This van drives pretty smooth," Oskar remarked. He obviously didn't want to discuss women anymore. "The tank also seems quite full. So, purely theoretically speaking, we could—"

"No," Tina cut in.

"Maybe there's another branch of this church in Husum?" Markus suggested.

"That's ridiculous. Absolutely not!" Tina plucked at her black blouse. Her shirt was starting to smell sweaty, much to her annoyance. "You two can just forget that. The man helped us, and besides, we aren't criminals."

Oskar snorted with laughter. Markus joined in.

"I really mean that."

"Sorry, Tina, but you have to admit that your last remark fell a little short of the truth." Markus grinned at her in the rearview mirror, and despite her best effort, a quick smile flashed across her face.

"Okay, you're right. But regardless, we're going to take this van to where it belongs."

"We wouldn't actually be stealing it," Oskar pointed out. "We would give it back, just in a different location, so to speak."

"No. The man trusted us, and we aren't going to take advantage of that. Besides, there are so few truly selfless people these days. I think that, in honor of the pastor, we should do something good too."

"I'm not setting up a charity organization or joining some monastery," Oskar declared firmly. "Monks sleep on very hard beds, and they probably don't have cable TV or warm water. Instead, they get bald helipads on their heads. Well, if you want to be specific, I have one, too, but you can still just forget about that. I've spent ninety years avoiding that path."

"I thought you were eighty-seven," Markus shot back.

"You bet I am," Oskar growled.

"That's not what I meant anyway. No, it's quite simple. For example, we could . . ." Tina peered out the window, looking for something that would make her idea more concrete. They were once again passing a few cows. Didn't they look sad, lonely, and pleading, troubled by flies and driven to bovine insanity by the meat industry? She had been through so much craziness over the past twenty-four hours that nothing could shock her by this point. Why not suggest something completely insane? "For example, we could free a few cows from their industrial farm. Maybe those over there."

"Those over there?" Markus remarked, amused. "The three cows over there in the meadow? The ones happily chomping on grass?"

"Oh, they'll be thrilled," Oskar said. "And what would you want to do with them? Should we squeeze them into the third row behind you? And would they actually be grateful to come along for the ride?" Oskar pretended to talk like a mooing cow. "Hi, I'm Bessie, and this is Rosie, and she's Daisy. We are Scottish Highland cows. Thank you for freeing us. Daisy, scoot over a little, my dear. You're getting a little chubby. Stop squishing my udder, or I'll end up flooding the van."

Tina broke into laughter. "No, well . . . Okay, then . . ." Something else caught her eye. "Up there! Look! We could pick up those hitchhikers." She leaned back in triumph. In reality, there were two people standing on the edge of the road with their thumbs out. Did people actually still do that these days? Two teenagers, they realized as they drew closer. A few years younger than Paul. Tina guessed that they were fifteen or sixteen. Goodness, they were still kids! To her deep satisfaction, Markus slowed down.

"They look fairly young," he said.

"Then we definitely need to pick them up."

"Okay." Markus came to a stop in front of the couple.

"And now we'll just hope that these aren't two eager-beaver scouts on the hunt for some criminals," Oskar muttered under his breath.

Crap. In her quest to do something good, Tina hadn't even thought about that. However, as the two teens approached, she felt less worried. They didn't look as if they had spent the entire day tirelessly watching the news. The boy had a few piercings, and there was some kind of pattern shaved into his hair. The girl's hair was dyed henna red. Her eyes were teary, and her shirt had a large spot on it.

"Hey, man, thanks. We've been standing out here forever, but nobody would stop," the boy said in greeting. "Julie has a blister and can't walk any more. Where are you going?"

"Würzburg," Markus replied.

"Low-key cool. That's where we're going, aren't we, Julie?"

"Thank you." The girl named Julie wiped her face, then the two of them climbed into the van and sat next to Tina.

"Oh, man, it burns like crazy." Julie pulled her foot up, and Tina caught sight of a huge red blister on her heel.

"Ouch!" she exclaimed. "I can tell that hurts."

"Look at what Grandpa Oskar found in the glove box." Oskar held up a package of bandages and handed it to the back seat.

"Thanks, Gramps. Hey, it's really great that we met you." The boy tore open the package, pulled out a bandage, and carefully treated his girlfriend's foot. He then slipped his arm around her, pulled her against him, kissed her hair, and whispered something comforting into her ear.

Tina could hardly take her eyes off the young couple. They were so young and so . . . in love. They couldn't keep their hands off each other and were pressed together as tightly as Velcro. Tina could only vaguely recall what this stage of things had felt like. In the rearview mirror, her eyes met Markus's. He had seen them too. She quickly averted her gaze.

"How did you end up on this back road?" she asked the two teens. She wasn't really interested in the answer, but the lovey-dovey whispering was surprisingly hard to bear.

"That's a long story," the boy murmured. "We've been on the road for two days."

"Ran away from home, did you?" Oskar guessed.

"Something like that." Julie sounded defiant as she snuggled even closer to her boyfriend.

"Don't worry. We won't rat you out." He smiled at the two of them. "I'm running away, too, just not from my parents."

A smile slipped across the girl's face.

"They actually weren't all that bad," Oskar continued. "At some point, they even realized that I didn't want to work in insurance like my father. I preferred photography."

"You were lucky," the girl said. "My parents just don't get it. They can't stand Roman because of his hair, and because he isn't good in school. But what's so bad about that?"

"My dad is the same," the boy cut in. "Don't do this, don't do that. But we aren't letting anyone tell us what to do anymore."

"What grade are you in?" Tina asked the girl.

"I'm in tenth, but it's hard for me. My parents want me to study all sorts of things. They keep coming up with new stuff for me to do, like going overseas and junk like that. So annoying."

"What do you want to do?" Tina asked cautiously. She felt a moment of déjà vu. Hadn't she recently had a similar conversation with Paul? Hadn't she insisted that he finish his AP classes, despite the fact it was extremely hard for him?

"Something with animals. Open an animal sanctuary or something like that. Roman could build it." The two of them locked eyes as they held hands.

"Our son is also having a hard time in school," Tina heard herself say, much to her surprise. "He isn't interested in college and wants to go into boatbuilding instead."

"What?" Markus whipped his head around and stared at Tina. "This is the first I've heard that."

"Hey! Eyes on the road, young man!" Oskar grabbed the steering wheel, barely preventing them from landing in the ditch.

"Boatbuilding? Wow, that's cool! So neat that you're letting him do that," Julie cried with admiration.

"Uh . . . thanks," Tina muttered.

Markus shot her a horrified look in the rearview mirror. "Boatbuilding? Are you kidding?" he mouthed.

"I just wish my parents would leave me alone." Julie sighed.

"Forget about them." Roman hugged her. "We'll do our own thing."

"Boy, I'm glad I'm not young anymore," Oskar remarked. "True, a few of my body parts could stand being twenty years younger. But not as young as you folks. The stress you're going through today, that's not for me. The entire world is open to you. The huge range of options out there these days is enough to drive you crazy. You keep wondering if you chose the wrong thing."

"Exactly, Grandpa." Julie nodded as she played with the turquoise pendant on her necklace.

"I don't feel like I've made the wrong decision." Roman tightened his arm around Julie. "Even if our parents don't agree."

Suddenly, Tina visualized her mother's face. "What? You want to marry Markus?" she had asked Tina in astonishment, as if her daughter had just announced that she wanted to marry the scion of some Mafia family. "But, Tina, a man like that isn't husband material!"

"Oh, is that what you think?" Tina had been so furious, she felt she might explode. How narrow-minded! All because Markus wasn't the ambitious businessman in a suit and tie that her mother had always dreamed about. "I'll show you that he's husband material!" And she actually did, two weeks later, secretly and alone at the marriage license office. She had worn a fire-red satin dress and carried a bouquet of white lilacs. It had been the most rebellious thing Tina had ever done in her life, driven by her deep inner sense that Markus and she were meant for each other and that he would do anything for her.

All of a sudden, it was clear to her that he had undertaken the holdup at the gas station in a moment of pure hopelessness, spurred by resignation and anger that he had never actually achieved anything in his life. Out of his love for her and Paul, he had acquired that dumb toy pistol and stormed into that gas station in blind desperation.

For a while, they drove on in silence. Julie snuggled against her boyfriend and squinted into the sun. Markus concentrated on driving. Oskar hunted for a radio station and finally found a Beatles song that he then hummed along with. Tina remained wrapped in her thoughts until they reached the city limits of Würzburg. She wondered if she would pick Markus a second time, if she could turn back time. She would—

"Shit," Markus cursed. "Do you see that up there?"

"Turn around," Oskar ordered instantly.

"Wha—" Tina started, but then she saw it. Hardly fifty yards away, there was a traffic block. It had been set up behind a curve, a strategically clever spot where clueless speeders would slip into the officer's net like fat carp. A cop was waiting in front of the patrol vehicle, looking their way.

"Too late," Markus hissed. "He's waving us down."

The cop was signaling for them to come closer.

"Drive into the field!" Tina leaned forward and wished she could take the wheel from him. "Markus, floor it. Otherwise, we're done for!"

"You mean that field with all the sunflowers? The ones I'd smash flat like a lawnmower? Yeah, we'd get far going that way." He gripped the steering wheel tighter. "Shitshitshit." They rolled to a stop alongside the policeman.

Tina looked at the sunflower field and the summery landscape, inhaling the scent of grass and freedom one last time. She glanced, almost tenderly, at the young couple, who were now unentangling themselves and looking around in surprise. Adieu, freedom—hello, women's prison! Maybe she'd at least get a nice cellmate, a robust, strong individual who could help defend her against the unavoidable beatings in the shower room in exchange for Tina teaching her to read and write. Tina could already imagine her future life. At the prison Christmas party, she would listen to the very first poem ever composed by that world-weary woman:

> The tinsel shines against the tree
> behind these bars, I'm still not free . . .

"Hello, driver's license and vehicle registration, please."

Tina flinched. The policeman had knocked on the window. Markus opened it, his hands shaking as he did so. He nodded at the officer, then acted as if he were searching for his wallet.

"Hi there," Oskar piped up. "Has there been a problem?"

Delaying the inevitable, Tina thought in despair. The policeman now leaned a little farther and peered into the vehicle. He suddenly looked startled. "I can't believe it!" he exclaimed. "Who do we have here?"

Tina opened her mouth, spontaneously deciding, in an act of insane heroism, to confess to everything, when someone else got the first word in.

"Dad?"

"Roman, what in the world are you doing in there? Do you have any idea how worried Mom has been?" The officer now opened the door, ignoring the completely baffled Markus, who was still almost robotically patting around on his shirt as if convinced his driver's license was located somewhere between the first and third missing buttons.

"Dad, we ran away because you all keep picking on us and never leave us alone. And Julie's parents—"

"Julie's parents are scared out of their minds. They came over yesterday, and I had the hardest time convincing them that filing a missing person's report wasn't necessary."

"We saw the young runaways and thought we'd give them a lift. Julie can't walk anymore, thanks to her blisters." Oskar gave the officer a chummy smile. "Don't be too hard on these two. We were all innocent and young, once upon a time. I just happen to still be that way."

"What? Sure. Thanks." The officer just glanced at him, as if he couldn't quite make him out. "Now get out, you two," he said, turning back toward his son. "We'll call Julie's parents, and then, for God's sake, come home! We won't do anything to you."

Tina almost felt sorry for the man as he stood there, exhausted and shaking his head in the summer heat. Beads of sweat had formed on his forehead, and his uniform was a little too tight. The challenge of raising kids was the same no matter who you were. Roman and Julie took as long as possible to extract themselves from their seats and climb out of the van as coolly as they could manage.

"Hi, son." The officer wrapped his arms around the boy. "Hi, Julie." He also pulled the girl in for a quick hug. The two teens squirmed sheepishly in his arms.

"Well, we'll just get going now," Oskar called out to the policeman. He waved a piece of paper in his direction, which he had obviously found somewhere. "Do you still need the license and registration?"

"No, no! All good. Safe travels!" The officer waved them off without even looking back at them.

"Go," Tina whispered. "Just go."

Markus finally stopped patting down his shirt and started the engine.

"And now cheerful waves, you two," Oskar murmured. *"Who's riding so late where winds blow wild? It is old Oskar with your child,"* he quipped, deliberately adapting a line from a famous poem.

Tina and Markus waved as stiffly as North Korean government officials while Oskar unfolded the "driver's license." "Coffee hour with Jesus, every Wednesday afternoon at 3:00 p.m. at Parish House South," he read aloud. "Too bad we missed that."

"Whew," Markus groaned. "I can't believe it. That was close."

"And all because we picked up Romeo and Juliet. Your idea, Tina. My respect." Oskar took one last look at the two teens, now standing like drenched poodles in front of Roman's father as he talked into his phone, their hands tightly linked. "Just look at them. The first love is always the most beautiful. And the last love is the true one."

"And what about those that fall in between?" Tina wondered.

"Well, you have to find that out yourself."

"There isn't any *in between*," Markus said. "There is only *one* true love."

Tina felt something come loose inside her. What had he just said? More precisely—when had he last said something like that to her? It felt like it had been decades.

"You think so?" Their eyes met once more in the rearview mirror, and this time, Tina didn't look away.

"I do. And over there are the outskirts of Würzburg. All we have to do now is find Parish House South. And then I'll drink a very personal cup of coffee with Jesus. Or maybe a beer would be better. Man, that was stressful!"

They crossed what felt like countless roads until they reached a quieter neighborhood, which almost looked rural. Tina asked a woman out walking her dachshund where Parish House South was located, and a few minutes later, they reached their destination. A small white church adjacent to a graveyard, a parish hall, a restaurant, a dentist's office, and a couple of small row houses.

"All right." Markus parked next to the parish hall and pulled out the car key. "Now what?"

"We have to get a new car," Oskar decided. "And I know exactly where to do that." He pointed casually out the window. "There are plenty of options over there."

In the parking lot in front of the church were all sorts of cars, the owners of which were in the process of shouting congratulations at a bridal couple who were being showered with rice as they stepped out of the church.

"You want to steal a car at a wedding?" Tina asked in horror.

Oskar shrugged. "Better than a funeral, I'd say. Besides, in about an hour, they'll all be so snockered that they won't be able to drive anyway."

He was right. Again. "Okay." Tina got out of the van. "Follow me, you scoundrels!"

11

The wedding guests numbered at least one hundred individuals who were excitedly milling around in front of the church. Nobody paid Tina, Oskar, and Markus even the slightest attention as they hurried across the parking lot, glancing around like they were looking for their parked car.

"Well? See anything?" Markus whispered to Oskar.

"No. No open windows. Everything's locked. Is this a wedding for insurance agents, or what?" Slightly irritated, Oskar rolled past a dark-blue Audi and nonchalantly checked the doors. He shook his head. "We'll need to find another solution."

"How?" Tina asked. She was slowly starting to feel uneasy. Hadn't someone just now looked at them suspiciously?

"Let's mingle among those folks," Oskar suggested, pointing at the wedding guests. "In case anyone asks, you're Andrea, Uncle Achim's third wife's second cousin. You and your husband are absolutely delighted to finally be able to meet everyone. You've heard so much about your relations, et cetera, et cetera."

"What?" Tina asked in confusion. "Who am I?"

"Exactly. Nobody will get it. Your story will be too complicated and will squelch all questions. And I'm Uncle Heinrich. Let's go!"

"But why?" Tina still didn't understand what he wanted to get out of this.

"Car keys." A glow extended across Markus's face. "Oskar wants to steal car keys, right?"

"Kudos to you, my boy. You're being promoted from assistant kidnapper to accomplice. A suitable raise will come later. Let's go. They're taking pictures now, all squeezed in tight. We won't get a better opportunity."

Putting on her poker face, Tina pushed Oskar's wheelchair into the wedding gathering, with Markus in tow. In her two-day-old blouse, she felt much too grubby for an occasion like this; besides, she felt uncertain about the whole affair. They were bound to all know each other and would immediately know that Tina, Markus, and Oskar didn't belong to the family. However, just a few moments later, she had to admit that Oskar was outstanding in his part.

"Man, you've grown so much, my boy!" he shouted to a completely unknown teenager, who was standing around in his stiff dark-blue suit and sullenly staring at his phone. "Spitting image of your father. But where is he? I don't see him."

Tina held her breath. What if this boy's father wasn't here? What if his parents were divorced, or if he was an orphan or a child adopted from Moldova? Or if his unknown father was a number in some refrigerator attached to a fertility clinic? These days, anything was possible! Oskar was playing with fire here.

The boy reluctantly looked up from his phone. "He's over there." He pointed at a short, balding man with a paunch, whom the boy didn't resemble in the slightest.

"Ah, your father isn't getting any younger, is he?" Oskar quipped.

"Don't let Harry hear you!" a woman in a lilac dress exclaimed with a laugh. Stepping out of the crowd behind the boy, she moved close to Oskar.

"Come on! Harry has always had a sense of humor! He and I go way back. I remember changing his diapers. Even then he had a bald spot." Oskar giggled. "Anyway, I need to get going so I can chat with the others." He nodded at a group of strangers, who automatically nodded back. "Push me over there," he whispered to Tina. "They won't notice us joining them."

Against a lushly blooming rosebush next to the church steps, a photographer was messing around with his tripod and camera as he tried to get the guests to assemble in photogenic groups. This seemed to be a rather difficult task, since a horde of children who were supposed to be included were fidgeting and acting up. The photographer took a step back to try to get everyone in the picture. He was standing on the topmost step with his back to the roses when it happened, so fast that nobody could intervene. One of the restless children raced up the steps, lightning fast and without watching where he was going, and rammed into the photographer. With a startled shout and a desperate attempt to keep his balance, the man tumbled down the steps.

A shout went through the crowd. The photographer tried to climb to his feet at the bottom of the steps but was completely dazed. He gave up and stayed seated, holding his head. As blood trickled down his face, the group of guests set itself in motion. Someone dashed off, someone else fetched a compress, and a few minutes later, two men appeared with a stretcher. They loaded up the photographer and carried him off. As the excitement subsided, the bride could be heard quietly complaining.

"I *told* you I wanted to have Oliver Keilmann do the photographs, not that strange guy," she ranted to her brand-new husband. "Oliver shoots all the celebrities and knows his stuff. He wouldn't have fallen down in the middle of everything!"

"But, sweetie, Mike just stumbled. Anyone could—" The new husband, upset, tried to defend his friend, but he wasn't allowed to finish his thought.

"Nobody's allowed to stumble on my wedding day!" The bride was growing increasingly peevish. "This is supposed to be the best day of my life!"

"Don't panic! Make way for Uncle Heinrich!" Oskar called out.

To Tina's dismay, he stood up from his wheelchair, strode over to the tripod, and secured the camera back onto it. She couldn't believe what she was seeing. Oskar actually seemed a little more stable on his feet now. What had happened to the delicate Mr. Krauss with a double *s* from the day before?

"Now, all the kiddos need to push together. Whoever wants ice cream afterward needs to shout *Here!*"

"Here!" the children screeched, laughing.

And from that moment on, it was as if Oskar was a different man. His movements were fluid, and his eyes were sharp. He chattered a blue streak. The other guests laughed at his remarks, and he made the children squeal for joy and the old ladies giggle coyly. Somehow he magically transformed the herd of boorish, beer-bellied men into a row of well-mannered gentlemen. Even the grumbling bride smiled and beamed once more as Oskar showered her with compliments and allowed her to strike the most outlandish poses for him.

Tina watched him nervously and clutched Markus's hand as she forced herself to smile and nod all around.

"Why is he doing this?" she asked. "Now they're really going to notice us. And this isn't helping him steal any keys."

"Don't know." Markus fell silent for a moment. "Maybe it just feels good to be taking pictures again?"

Tina said nothing. She should have thought of that herself. The fact that Oskar was no longer employed as a photographer didn't mean he didn't miss that work. And you could tell that he was fully in his element. He was hardly limping anymore.

"Heidi's Jonas really is a little rascal, isn't he?" a voice next to Tina piped up.

Tina winced and gazed into the rigid, unwrinkled face of a woman in her late forties. Her lipstick was purple, and her platinum-blond hair was topped with a flat, white hat and veil. With her hat, yellow outfit, and white gloves, she reminded Tina of Dustin Hoffman and his protective suit in *Outbreak*. An athletically built man stood next to the woman. He was reading a text on his phone and grinning appreciatively. The woman cocked her eyebrows, probably to underscore the fact that by *rascal* she didn't mean some cute little boy but a spoiled, bratty nightmare of a child.

"Oh, yes. Jonas . . ." Tina repeated, completely ignorant of whom they were discussing.

"I mean, Heidi didn't even apologize to the poor man. He might have a concussion! But Jonas is being raised rather freely . . ." At this point, the woman batted her eyes meaningfully, although her forehead didn't move at all. "And we all know what that means, don't we? And of course Heidi doesn't want to miss the cold buffet, although it wouldn't exactly hurt her to do so."

What a poisonous witch! But at least Tina now knew whom the woman was talking about.

"I'm Katie, the groom's aunt. And who are you?" the woman wanted to know.

"I'm Andrea, the second cousin of Uncle Achim's third wife. And this is my husband." Tina obediently recited what Oskar had told her to. Nonetheless, she now started to sweat. "And that is Uncle Heinrich." She pointed at Oskar.

The woman closed one eye and studied Oskar. "Isn't that the man whose wife passed away? What was it, Heiner? Wasn't it a stroke?"

"How the hell would I know?" the man next to her growled. He then eyed Tina and Oskar thoughtfully. "You do look familiar to me."

"Isn't Uncle Achim the brother of Jürgen?" the woman continued to prod.

"Yes, he's Jürgen's brother, exactly. He was . . . is . . ." Tina started to stutter, but fortunately someone else called out at that moment.

"Champagne over here!"

Tina and Markus were suddenly surrounded by a throng of people, who were all streaming into the restaurant next to the church.

"What are we supposed to do now?" Tina whispered to Markus.

He glanced around, searching. "You should follow them. I'll take care of Oskar."

~

Tina nonchalantly took a seat at the bar and sipped on a glass of champagne that someone handed her. Every time she saw a white hat bobbing close by, she dove for cover. Markus finally came into view. He was pushing Oskar, who was enthroned once more in his wheelchair.

"Did you get a key?" Tina looked around. "It's time we got out of here."

"Not yet. And Oskar is supposed to take more photos."

"Well, they'll need to find someone else. We—"

"But Oskar does it the best." Markus gave her a strange look that she couldn't interpret.

Tina squinted at him in confusion, but then she understood. This was Oskar the professional photographer—and not the mobility-challenged Mr. Krauss from the Sonnenberg Assisted Living Community. Oskar wanted to stay longer. How selfish of her. One hour wouldn't make a difference one way or the other.

"Okay," she said. "Just keep that annoying woman in the white hat away from me. And her awful husband, who keeps watching us."

"We'll handle that." Oskar rubbed his hands together. "Take me over there, my boy."

While Oskar and Markus moved toward the unpleasant man, Tina's gaze slid over to the TV hanging above the bar. She froze. A photo of her was flickering on the screen! As was one of Markus and the word WANTED. Tina quickly scanned her surroundings. Dammit! Had anyone noticed? It didn't look like it. Nobody was paying any attention to the news.

Her picture was now gone from the screen, but a woman that Tina knew all too well had taken its place. It was Susi, her childhood friend! Susi, the buttoned-up killjoy with the high-ranking police job. Had someone asked her to get involved with this case? If so, they were all in trouble, because Susi was incredibly thorough and unyielding, and wherever her work was concerned, she knew no friends. Tina leaned forward and listened.

". . . today the family of the kidnapping victim . . . later . . . an appeal to the culprits . . . on television . . . ask for help . . ."

"Want another drink?" The barkeeper tore her out of her thoughts.

"Yes, thank you," Tina replied with presence of mind as she waved her glass to distract the man. Susi finally vanished from the screen. Tina exhaled and fled to the restroom. She set her purse down on the sink and spritzed her face with water.

The door opened behind her. It was Katie, the woman with the white hat.

"Well?" Her eyes glittered with a joy that bordered on malice. "Have you been enjoying yourselves?"

"Totally." Tina pumped the poor soap dispenser hard, as if it owed her money. "It's been a truly beautiful wedding."

"Hannah was his second choice, you know," the woman confessed to Tina.

"Ah."

"Tim wanted to marry someone else, but she turned him down. Oh well, they're a handsome couple, nonetheless. Just a question of how long." The woman coughed.

"Hopefully forever, Katie." What a bitch. "That's the whole point of getting married, isn't it? How long have you been married?"

Katie's eyes narrowed to slits. "Is Uncle Achim here too?" she shot back. "You really must introduce me to him."

The two women sized each other up as if they were about to shoot it out in front of a Wild West saloon.

"Unfortunately, he couldn't come," Tina retorted smoothly. "Advanced diabetes. He rarely leaves home these days. But he would've loved to meet you. It's a shame." She rinsed her hands and quickly ripped off a mouse-gray paper towel.

"Indeed. But Uncle Jürgen must be here, right?" Katie took a very small step toward Tina, which Tina countered with a very small step backward.

At that moment, the door swung open, and a cluster of bridesmaids fluttered in. They immediately filled the space with laughter and chirping chatter, and Tina used the opportunity to slip out of the restroom. Oskar and Markus were waiting outside, thank goodness.

"Everything okay?" she asked nervously as she joined them.

"Just fine. Mrs. Veil's husband is busy right now hunting for his phone. Here." Oskar slipped something into Tina's purse. "I was standing next to him when he entered his passcode. People my age tend to be invisible these days—a fact that has its advantages. He'll miss out on his latest Tinder picks, but that's just the way it goes. Now you can give Paul a call."

"You didn't . . ."

"What, what? Just be happy. Give Paul a call and whoever else you want. Do you have family in the States? Colombia? Somewhere expensive to call. I really dislike men who cheat on their wives, even if their spouses happen to be annoying biddies like our old girl with a hat. By the way, she's heading this way."

The awful Katie was steaming toward them, this time with a gaunt man in tow. What did this snake want from them now? She had grown suspicious, that much was certain.

"Here is Uncle Jürgen," Katie called out while they were still about six feet away. "But he was just telling me that he doesn't have a brother named Achim. So, you're going to need to explain to me exactly which Achim you mean." She smiled like the Cheshire cat.

"Uh, I feel rather dizzy," Oskar groaned, swiftly undoing the top button of his shirt. "Please roll me out to get some fresh air. Right away, children!"

Tina and Markus simultaneously reached for the wheelchair handles. "Uncle Heinrich, you shouldn't run around so much. Remember your blood pressure! This is what you get. Excuse us!" Tina shoved the wheelchair forward, right over Katie's toes. Katie yelped.

"We'll be right back. Uncle needs his heart medicine, which is in the car. Isn't it, uncle, dear?" Markus bellowed.

He and Tina exchanged a smile, unnoticed by everyone. When was the last time they had spent so much time together without arguing about money or household stuff or something else? On a whim, she planted a kiss on her husband's lips as they stepped outdoors. He raised his eyebrows. "Well now, young woman. Just wait until I tell Uncle Achim!"

"It would be better if you told Uncle Heinrich." Tina was starting to enjoy this. "After all, he isn't doing well, you know." She leaned down to Oskar. "Right, Uncle Hein—"

Sweat was beading across Oskar's forehead. His face was white, and his eyes were half closed. He was slumped limply in his wheelchair. "Oskar? Oskar, what are you doing? You can stop. We're outside now."

Oskar didn't react. He just squinted a little.

He wasn't playing. Oh God, he wasn't playing at all. He really was feeling bad. Tina opened her mouth, but her voice failed her.

"Oskar?" Markus grabbed the old man's hand and glanced up at Tina. "It's ice cold."

12

Tina felt panic rise within her. "Markus, what do we do now? Does he need a doctor? Should we call an ambulance?"

Oskar moved his lips, murmuring something.

"What?" Markus knelt down close to him and patted his hand. "What is it, Oskar?"

"No ambulance. I'll never ever get into one of those things with you two hoodlums again."

Tina laughed, although it sounded more like a sob. He was alive! He was still himself, cracking jokes again. "God, Oskar, you scared us. What is going on with you?"

"Just a little dizzy." Oskar tried to sit up straight but failed. "I need to lie down for a bit. It was all a little overwhelming. Don't need a doctor. He'd just call the police. Or even worse—my son-in-law or the bulldog of a head nurse at my old facility."

"But . . ." Tina bit her lip. *But what if it happens again?*

She leaned against Markus as he pulled a handkerchief out of his pants pocket and wiped off Oskar's forehead.

"I'll get him a glass of water." Markus stood up.

"No, I want some brandy," Oskar croaked after him.

Tina held the old man's hand. A little color was returning to his face, at least.

"Man, Oskar," she said as it suddenly dawned on her how deeply she cared for this small, crazy old man. God forbid something happen to him. He was the one who had brought a spark back to their lives. He took everything that came his way with humor and embodied the exact opposite of their habitual drabness, their tedious jobs, and their daily frustration.

"I'm feeling better," Oskar insisted. Markus returned with a glass of water and handed it to him.

Tina shook her head. "No, you should lie down for an hour or so."

However, the very next moment, she realized how pointless her order was; there were no beds available for him. They didn't even have a car, and there was no telling when they would be able to "organize" another vehicle. Even if someone were to give them a car in the next ten minutes (which was extremely unlikely—Tommy Hilfiger was more likely to include Fashion World's dull pieces in his fall collection), they wouldn't reach Husum until midnight. If they actually got there. Such a long trip with Oskar in his condition . . .

Tina looked around. There had to be some place around here where a person could lie down. She glanced at the restaurant they had just left. Like an insidious beekeeper, Katie with her veiled hat was lingering at the window and staring out at them. A mischievous smile flitted across her face. She waved at Tina and held something aloft. Tina froze. It was her bulging purse, which she had left sitting in the restroom.

"Crap, Markus, we have to get out of here. That irritating woman found my purse in the restroom, and there's no way she hasn't opened it. That kind of person always opens everything they find. And now there's nothing in the world she wants more than to talk to me about all those bills and coins. My ID happens to be in there as well. Double crap!"

"But our money . . ." Markus stammered, taken aback. He took a step toward the restaurant.

"Stop!" Tina grabbed his arm. "That was never our money, Markus. It's the gas station's money. It never belonged to us—you understand?"

"But then we're back to being completely broke. What are we supposed to do next?"

"Nothing. We can't go back in there. Let's set off on a slow, casual stroll, as if we just want to get some fresh air." Tina paused and took an exaggerated sniff from a flower on one of the bushes in front of the church.

"She's right. We'll figure out something else," Oskar murmured weakly.

"Come on." Tina set off without looking back at the conniving Katie, who had to be wrenching her thrice-nipped-and-tucked neck to watch them. No, there was no way they could go back there, even if they hadn't been able to snag any car keys. And as far as the money was concerned, it was now of secondary importance—Oskar was much more important. He urgently needed to lie down and recover, but where? Maybe there was a park where someone could stretch out if necessary. Or a—

"A hotel," she decided spontaneously as she pointed straight ahead. There, across the street, a sign indicated a hotel about a hundred yards away. "That. The Castle Augustin Hotel. Let's go in there and sit down in the lobby. They usually have air conditioning and soft, pretty chairs. We'll just act as if we're waiting on someone, and Oskar can rest a while. Come on, let's go!"

~

The Castle Augustin Hotel was an elegant, top-class hotel, Tina realized with astonishment as they stepped through the entrance. This was a place of whispers and lowered voices. Long-legged desk clerks with velvety skin and beaming smiles stood at the check-in desk like creatures from the planet of eternal youth and beauty. A planet to which Tina would never even receive a landing permit, because when she caught sight of herself and Markus and Oskar in the huge wall mirror, her stomach dropped.

"We look absolutely dreadful!" she hissed at Markus as she smoothed her blouse, which by now clung to her like crepe paper.

In addition, a wire in her bra had worked itself free and was poking her with every breath she took. Her hair stood out from her head like a frizzy cloud, and her shoes were covered in dust from their walk along the country road. Markus looked even worse. His shirt was missing almost all of its buttons, and he had a five-o'clock shadow across his cheeks and a food spot on his pants, presumably from breakfast that morning. And then there was Oskar in his squeaky wheelchair, his skin ashen as if he were just about to have or had just had a heart attack. They resembled refugees from the waning days of World War II, whom it had taken decades to struggle through the dense, unforgiving forests of Poland and who, due to mysterious circumstances, had only now reached civilization once more, here of all places.

"So what? The cool air feels good. Let's sit down over there by the fountain," Markus said. "They even have pillows on those seats. If we can act super self-confident, they'll think we're some kind of crazy rock stars or something."

"Of course. Everyone will come running and ask for our autographs," Tina murmured, but she nonetheless pushed Oskar's wheelchair over to a comfortable-looking couch. She helped the old man onto it, before collapsing into the upholstery, spent. About six feet away sat a businessman in a pale-gray suit. He looked up in irritation, then immediately glanced back down at his laptop.

"Ah, this pillow is doing wonders for my aching backside," Oskar groaned. "And if you could help me out of my shoes and find me a bandage for my corn, my dear, I would be ever so grateful."

The man in the suit looked up again, and this time he wrinkled his nose as he watched Tina help Oskar out of his slippers. The man cleared his throat audibly.

Oskar couldn't have cared less, since at that moment, Markus reappeared with three bottles of water he'd found somewhere. Tina tried to fold up the wheelchair, but it decided to be stubborn and wouldn't cooperate. It slipped out of her hands, and with a loud clatter, it raced toward the man in the suit and gave him a nudge, as if it wanted to invite him to play.

The man shot them an annoyed look and pushed the wheelchair away with his elbow so he didn't have to touch it with his hands. "Can't you be more careful?" he said, with a snort in her direction.

Tina felt herself growing mad. What a jerk! Who did he think he was?

The man's phone now went off. "Hello? Ah no, I'm still at the hotel. The Castle Augustin. It's really heading downhill. It's unbelievable, the kind of people they let in these days. Please don't book me in here again." The look he gave them was poisonous. "Hm. Hm. Ah." The man opened up his briefcase and rummaged around in it. "Yes, I got the rental car. What a joke. They gave me a Jeep. In jungle green! Am I some kind of game hunter? I had requested a BMW—unbelievable. Don't ever use that company again. No, of course I'm not driving it around. I've left it sitting in front of the hotel. They're supposed to bring me a replacement. And my Miles & More card with Lufthansa seems to be expiring soon." The man pulled a wallet out of his jacket and opened it. "I don't know anything about it. That's *your* responsibility. Yes, that's what the notification said—expiring." He pulled out a card and studied it angrily. "Take care of it!"

Tina could no longer take it. "Oskar," she whispered, "are you feeling any better? We need your help."

"It depends on what you're planning. If you want to tango, I'll have to disappoint you." As if to demonstrate his point, Oskar tried to stand up, but he didn't get far and slipped right back down onto the couch.

"No, no, no worries. Can you share a little of your . . . cleverness with us? I think the guy over there has way too many credit cards and way too little decency and humor."

"And we have way too few credit cards." He switched gears quickly. "That would be my pleasure, my dear. I know this kind of man all too well. When he was a kid, his mother hung a pork chop around his neck so at least the dog would play with him. Help me up and take me over there." He discreetly gestured toward the neighboring couch.

"Come on, Grandpa, we'll get you to your wheelchair," Markus declared loudly. "Obviously it isn't going to come back by itself." This was directed at the idiot in gray flannel, who seemed to be stricken with temporary deafness.

"On three." Oskar stood up and held on to Tina and Markus. "One." They moved slowly toward the wheelchair. "Markus, you take the key. Tina, the credit cards. Two." They were now standing practically on top of the man, who turned away from them in irritation and continued to shout into his phone.

"*Three.*" Oskar deliberately fell across the guy, who dropped his phone and wallet, while the briefcase clattered onto the floor.

"Are you insane? Be careful, dammit!" he bellowed, muffled by Oskar's body, while Tina shouted, "Grandpa, Grandpa, oh no!"

She deftly snatched the wallet off the floor, extracted three credit cards at random, and then dropped it again. Oskar threw his arms around the man and cried, "Pardon me! But my heart . . . oh . . . I can't breathe . . . !"

Markus pretended to pull Oskar away and, in the process, slipped his hand unnoticed into the man's jacket pocket. Everything happened in a heartbeat, and as the man furiously got to his feet and berated them, one of the pretty desk clerks rushed toward them in concern. Tina swiftly deposited her plunder into the wheelchair and settled Oskar on top of it.

"Oh, Grandpa," she exclaimed. "Are you feeling better now? And you," she snapped at the other man, "should be ashamed of yourself. Pushing a sick old man!"

"What?" the suit grunted, flushing dark red.

"I sincerely apologize," the desk clerk twittered, aghast. "The hotel manager will do everything to—"

"This is the last time we stay here!" Markus exclaimed with dignity. "The Castle Augustin really is going downhill. The kind of people hanging around here are concerning. We refuse to sit here and listen to ableist garbage." With a swift motion, he spun the wheelchair toward the exit.

"The sheer rudeness!" The man was about to explode. Tina noted with satisfaction that he was also now missing a button on his shirt.

"Goodbye." Tina nodded to the desk clerk, who was glancing from one to the other in confusion. The three of them then proceeded majestically out of the hotel.

"Do you have everything?" Tina asked Markus after they reached the sidewalk.

"Yep. And you?"

"I do too. Go get that car sitting over there, the pretty green Jeep."

"Got it." Markus strode off and drove up to the hotel drive a few minutes later. Tina watched the businessman through the hotel window; he was still talking to the desk clerk.

"What an idiot." Tina shook her head.

Oskar nodded. "Yep. He's a few fries short of a Happy Meal."

"Paul is always saying that too." Tina suddenly saw her son in her mind. Paul. She would call him next. She helped Oskar into the car and then climbed in herself. The last thing she saw before they drove off was the businessman, his face now raspberry pink as he shouted into his phone. The desk clerk was whispering with her colleague and discreetly tapping herself on the forehead.

~

"Paulie?"

"Mom, is that you? Did you get a new phone? Where are you? What's going on?"

"No, we just . . . found another phone. I'll explain everything to you soon. Are you doing all right? Do you have enough to eat? Have the cops done anything to you?"

Paul snorted in amusement. "*Found?* Yeah, right. Don't worry about me, I'm okay. Amelie's mom is cooking for me, and I'm stuffed. The cops were only here on the first day. They wanted to find out if I knew you were planning to hold up a gas station. Of course I didn't. There was nothing else they could do."

"I didn't know about it ahead of time either." Tina sighed. "Dad is a little . . ." She searched for a suitable description. Markus was listening in. "Dad kind of lost it for a moment. Everything went down the tubes that day and then came to a head. He just . . . He just . . ."

"I get it. Really do," Paul said, to her astonishment. He continued in a lower voice, "Sometimes I have days when everything just drives me nuts too." He cleared his throat. "But, uh, what did you do with the old man, Mom? Did you really . . . I mean, is he still alive? And where are you right now?"

"Of course he's still alive! His name is Oskar, and he's sitting up front next to Dad as we drive."

"Are you still in the car that belongs to that idiot from the news? The nurse from the care home? I saw all that."

"No, we now have a car from . . . another idiot." Suddenly, she was overcome by a fit of laughter and could hardly keep herself together. Everything was so absurd! "We're taking Oskar, the old man, home, to where he grew up. That's where he wants to go. He doesn't want to stay in the care home anymore. They aren't nice to him there, you know? And as soon as we get there, we'll call you and figure out where to meet you, and . . ." Tina fell silent. She shouldn't make promises she couldn't keep.

"Do you know that Susi woman is leading the investigation?" Paul now asked. "She came by and told me she was your friend and showed me an old photo of the two of you together and asked me all sorts of weird questions, like if we had relatives somewhere and if I knew where you might have gone. I didn't tell her anything, though. I'm not stupid. By the way, she's gained a ton of weight since whenever it was you were hanging out with her. I thought you might like to know that."

Tina smiled slightly. "Don't be mean."

"But it's true! And someone from a TV station stopped by too. They wanted me to come on a talk show." He paused for a moment. "I said yes, Mom. I need money, and they can't get anything out of me anyway. Some crazy older woman called as well. I think it was your boss. She was fussing because you hadn't called in sick. She wouldn't let me get a word in edgewise, so I just put the phone in the fridge for ten minutes. I hope that was okay?"

"Marvelous! Do you want to talk to Dad?"

There was a short pause. Tina couldn't blame him. The recent conversations between Paul and Markus, if you could even call them that, had typically ended in slamming doors.

"Okay," Paul finally said, albeit somewhat hesitantly.

"Markus, pull off to the right up there," Tina instructed her husband.

He parked in front of an office building, turned around, and took the phone from Tina, who listened in astonishment to the short but friendly conversation between father and son. Nobody shouted anything like "You just don't understand!" or "Man, I just can't understand you!"

One more thing they had to thank Oskar for.

13

"No, I'm all right, honestly," Oskar insisted when they pulled off on a side street a short time later because he was looking pale again. As things looked now, they might not be putting Würzburg behind them anytime soon. "And if you'll show me the credit cards belonging to our friend from the hotel, I'll feel much better."

Tina handed him the cards. What other options did she have? They couldn't just unload Oskar at a hospital and then speed away, like in an American thriller. Oskar was a proud man and couldn't be coerced into anything. They knew that much by now. As well as the fact that Oskar never would have put up with a mindless, humiliating job in a supermarket or at Fashion World. With his sense of humor, he would have wrapped everyone, including her dumb boss and *Mr.* Scheller, around his little finger and then made off with the year's profits.

"Looks good." Oskar seemed pleased. "Two Visa cards and some frequent-flyer thingy." He waved around a silver card. "Platinum Business Class Card," he read aloud. "This will allow you to be transported onto your plane on a litter carried by ten bodybuilders. And on the plane, they will have a silk-draped divan prepared for you, along with a personal masseuse and a chef who will wait on you, hand and foot, and fix you unicorn carpaccio and a peacock egg, and—"

"How good do the credit cards look?" Markus interrupted him cautiously.

"Considering that the guy scribbles his name as illegibly as a doctor, they look great! It will be easy to imitate his scrawl. There's nothing worse than a clean, neat signature."

"You sure?" Markus didn't sound convinced. "That could be true, but you're forgetting about the guy's photo on the card. I've never seen that before. A messy signature won't help us work around that."

"Far from it." Oskar held up the card. "Having a picture on it means that no nosy salesclerk will ask to see your ID, since they'll already have your photo."

"Nobody will ask *me*?" Markus repeated slowly.

"Yes, you. Who else can use this thing? I know I'm still quite youthful, dynamic, and handsome, but that guy happens to have a few more hairs on his head than me. And Tina's resemblance to him is rather limited."

"Thanks," Tina said.

"His hairstyle is completely different than mine," Markus protested.

"You have no hairstyle," she countered.

"But that guy's hair is slicked down and combed back behind his ears. And he's rocking that chiseled 'successful guy' chin, and his eyes are fishy. He has designer glasses, and as for his suit—"

"We'll work it out," Oskar said, brushing this off. "You just need to look as conceited as he does. Now get your noggin over here. I wanted to be a barber when I was a little boy."

"What are you cooking up?" Markus asked, alarmed. He leaned as far away from Oskar as his seat would allow. "Don't touch my hair! It used to be longer. I was so proud of it, and people used to tell me that I looked like the lead singer of Guns N' Roses, just so you know." He reached for the car door. He was obviously ready to push it open at any moment and flee into the little park across the street.

"Sure, and now you can look like Moby. His music isn't all that bad either."

Tina burst out laughing in the back seat.

"Don't worry, I'll just make a few improvements," Oskar continued. "So, first things first. Spit in my hand."

"Say what?" Markus scooted even farther away.

"Just do it," Oskar instructed. "Otherwise, I'll use my own spit. My mother always used to do that. One of my most traumatic childhood memories."

Markus reluctantly spit into Oskar's hand, who then started to smooth down Markus's hair and tuck it behind his ears.

"This was our trick years ago if we didn't have any hair gel," he told Tina. "And look what I found here." He pulled a pair of reading glasses out of his door pocket. "Some other corporate warrior left these behind. Here you go." He held the glasses out to Markus, who removed his own off-the-rack pair and set them aside. "Perfect."

Tina had to admit that Markus now actually did bear a certain resemblance to the photo on the credit card. The only things that didn't scan right were his pained expression and his tattered shirt. And Markus definitely couldn't manage the arrogance that the business windbag wore plastered on his face like a mask.

"And now let's go shopping," Oskar decided. "I desperately need a couple of corn bandages and something fresh to wear. And you, my boy, would benefit from a new shirt and a razor. Or are you planning to grow a beard?"

"Why not?" Markus laughed. "That would make a good disguise."

"But beards don't do anything for me," Tina pointed out.

"Really? You know that a man without a beard is like bread without a crust."

"If you say so, Oskar." Tina grinned. "In that case, I'll give the beard more thought, but only if Markus doesn't let it grow wild like a brambly hedge." Tina tugged at her blouse, the sight of which she could hardly stand anymore. "I'd really like something else to wear too. Come on, Markus. There's a department store over there." She pointed at the large red letters on the facade of a building on the other side of the small park.

Markus sighed. "Okay." Admitting defeat, he climbed out of the car. "But what about my outfit? I mean—the way I see it, no one is going to believe that I'm a successful executive."

"Just wait." Oskar rubbed his hands together. "We'll manage."

~

Once inside the store, Oskar immediately steered them toward the men's department. He decisively reached for a white button-down shirt and a light-gray suit, similar to what the guy at the hotel had been wearing.

Tina felt lightheaded when saw the price. She had never purchased such an expensive suit for Markus. With that sum, they would have preferred to pay for a month's groceries and the power bill. Besides that, Markus wouldn't have had any use for such elegant clothing. At work, he ran around in a light-blue apron with the supermarket's logo on it, and at home, he wore T-shirts paired with jeans or those awful sweatpants that he just couldn't seem to part with. When they went out in the evenings—which was a rare occurrence—they frequented places that didn't require them to dress up to get a schnitzel and beer.

"All right. Go try this on in the changing rooms over there," Oskar said. "And then go up to the checkout counter, specifically to the one with the frustrated woman with the botched haircut. Got it? Not to the one with the man. And you need to tell her that you want to wear the suit out of the store because you desperately need to get to a meeting and someone spilled coffee on your other one. When you say that, roll your eyes to emphasize the stupidity of your employees. Hurry up now!" He gave Markus a subtle shove. "And Tina, you chime in and act as if he is Andreas, your husband's coworker. That actually is the name of our chum on the credit card. And then ask him if he has met anyone new since his divorce—you haven't." This he directed at Markus. "I'll take care of the rest."

"How—" Markus began, but Oskar waved him off impatiently. "Just get going. You'll understand soon enough."

Markus headed off to the changing room, still uncertain, and soon reemerged.

"Wow." Tina's jaw dropped. He actually did look like the businessman from the hotel now, just nicer. He straightened up tall, took a deep breath, and headed toward the sales counter, behind which a middle-aged salesclerk with an absurdly asymmetrical haircut and a desperately youthful appearance yawned discreetly. At the sight of Markus, her eyes brightened.

"Afternoon, ma'am," Markus said gruffly. "I'd like to wear this suit out. Would you mind cutting off the tags? Someone from accounting just spilled coffee on my other suit." Markus rolled his eyes with exaggerated annoyance. "Let me tell you, sometimes your employees make you wish—"

"You're telling me." The clerk nodded in agreement, as if she had spent her whole life directing entire armies of stubborn employees all over the place.

"And I have this extremely important meeting coming up in ten minutes," Markus continued. He seemed to be growing more comfortable with his role.

"Oh, dear! I'd be glad to do that for you." The woman beamed at him and stepped out from behind her counter. Her skinny violet jeans were too tight, her hair roots dark, and her lipstick crumbly. Tina instantly recognized a kindred spirit. An underpaid, disillusioned woman of Tina's age, who was obviously lonely as well. She practically threw herself at Markus, and chattered away about how good he looked in the suit and how the fabric was both durable and luxurious. Time for Tina's entrance.

"Andreas?" she cried, acting surprised. "What are you doing here? I thought you'd be at that meeting with my husband by now."

"I'm on my way!" Markus gave her a firm banker's handshake. "And my flight to London leaves in four hours. I just needed to grab a new suit."

With growing enthusiasm, the clerk plucked invisible threads from his jacket.

"Yes, yes, the super-busy executive. Here today, gone tomorrow. After all, you don't have a family you have to take care of. I sometimes envy you singles." Tina tried to sound as envious as she possibly could. The clerk pricked up her ears.

"Have you met anyone yet?" Tina asked quietly, though not too quietly. The clerk was meant to hear what she said and, at the same time, think that she'd heard something she wasn't meant to.

"No." Markus flashed Tina a quick grin. "I'm still looking, but I'll find her, the woman of my dreams." He held the credit card out to the clerk. "I've got to run now. You have a nice selection here. I'll be back soon, I'm sure."

"Please do come back." The clerk beamed at him, before swiftly glancing at the card and running the charge. "That comes to nine hundred forty euros. Please sign here. The new fall fashions will be in next week, in case you might want to . . ." She left the rest of the sentence unspoken, as she suggestively fluttered her much-too-long eyelashes.

"Gladly. If I can rely on your charming advice." As if by accident, Markus brushed his little finger against the clerk's, who could hardly contain her enthusiasm.

"The suit really looks great on you," she stammered again. "Truly great." She handed him the receipt and hardly glanced at the signature.

"Oh my! I seem to have gotten lost in here," Oskar's voice suddenly sounded from somewhere between the Ralph Lauren pajamas and the Lacoste robes. "I was looking for the medical supply shop, but I seem to have passed through the wrong entrance. Where do I need to go?"

In the brief moment that the clerk was turned toward Oskar, Markus and Tina glided like shadows between the mannequins and the display tables.

The three of them met outside in front of the department store.

"You two were marvelous!" Oskar gave them a thumbs-up.

Tina agreed, although Markus had seemed, in her opinion, to have relished his role a tad too much. "Was it really necessary for you to touch her?"

"Jealous?" Markus shot back in lieu of a response and grinned. "I—"

"Now don't start quarreling over that poor soul back there," Oskar interrupted. "The main thing is that Markus now fully looks the part of our friend in the hotel. This will make our shopping easier, but we should continue our purchases somewhere else. And say, aren't you starting to get hungry?" He sniffed the air. "Something here smells delicious. Asian, perhaps. What would you think of Thai chicken in coconut milk? I think we should use credit card number two for that."

~

They bought a new dress and shoes for Tina, a casual shirt for Markus (because he loved them so much), and a few cosmetics, as well as a T-shirt bearing the words LEGEND IN RETIREMENT and corn bandages for Oskar.

With the business jerk's second credit card, they went out for Thai. It had been ages since Tina had eaten so well. She stuffed herself with peanut chicken and sauteed shrimp until she felt like she would explode. At that very moment, she could have hugged the world. The expensive wine made her feel lightheaded, and in a rush of exuberance after their meal, she tossed the frequent-flyer platinum business card into a travel agency's mailbox.

"Now our good man will have to stand in line at the airport and sit with his knees up to his ears in economy class, like all the rest of humanity." Oskar seemed delighted as he wiped his forehead with a handkerchief.

"Oskar?" Tina thought he was starting to look pale again. "Are you feeling all right?"

"I'm okay, I'm okay." He waved her off, but as he did so, he dropped his handkerchief because his hand was shaking. "Let's get out of here. I just had a little too much wine."

But Oskar hadn't drank all that much. Tina exchanged a concerned look with Markus. He gave his head an imperceptible shake.

"You know what?" She yawned. "I'm exhausted, and of course, Markus has drunk too much. We shouldn't drive any more today. Let's look for someplace around here to spend the night and get an early start tomorrow so we can reach Wobbenbüll in one day's drive."

"Good idea! There's no way I want to get on the wrong side of the law for drunk driving," Markus muttered.

Tina laughed, and Oskar joined in. "Marko, I see you're coming into your own."

"Markus." He rolled his eyes, but Tina could tell that he wasn't really mad.

And obviously Oskar was no longer opposed to relaxing somewhere for a night. The only question was where in the world they could put their feet up without attracting attention. Would a hotel scrutinize a credit card more closely than the salesclerk at the store? Probably. And what if the card had been blocked because of their lavish shopping spree? Would it set off an alarm somewhere? In terms of cash, they possessed exactly seventy-six euros and thirty cents—fifty euros from Oskar's pocket and the rest from Markus's notoriously meagre wallet. How far could they hope to get on that?

14

"Maybe a small B and B?" Markus suggested. They were driving around slowly and searching, without having come to any decisions. Markus now pulled off onto a small side street close to the downtown area.

Tina thought that a B and B would be too small, especially if a curious and talkative manager was waiting for potential guests to chat with from behind lace curtains. And then there would be the guests themselves—nothing but mutually bored married couples who, after countless years of lapsed chemistry in and out of bed, would welcome any distraction encountered on their vacation, particularly if that came in the form of a nationwide manhunt for kidnappers.

They weighed their options, and were already considering the advisability of breaking into the vocational school up on the corner and spending the night in the gym, wrapped in the fug of adolescent sweaty feet and sandwiched between medicine balls and wall bars, when Markus noticed a building farther down the street, through the doors of which streamed an array of backpacking young people, mostly Japanese from the look of it. He drove into the parking lot in front of the building and got out to ask what kind of place this was.

"It's a hostel," he declared happily. "Perfect. Not a soul in there will care about who we are. They're all staring at their phones, scrolling through social media. They aren't reading the news, and even if they did catch something about a gas-station holdup in Ingolstadt, they couldn't care less. And the hostel itself is cheap."

"Brilliant!" Tina exclaimed. And it really was brilliant. Because hostels were no longer limited to dorm-style rooms or solely characterized by herbal tea, rye bread, and long-haired night clerks who strummed their weathered guitars and crooned folk songs long after dark.

"Markus, you have a good mind. I herewith name you the acting head of our gang," Oskar said.

"And what should we call ourselves?" Markus gallantly opened Tina's door. "The Three Amigos?"

"The Ingolstadt Brotherhood?" Tina suggested.

"Simple—we're the Accidental Outlaws," Oskar said.

~

The young woman at the reception desk had artificially dyed black hair and a fire-breathing dragon tattooed on her arm. She looked exasperated and had obviously reached the limits of her communication abilities, which had nothing to do with the international guests and everything to do with her rudimentary knowledge of English, the language in which she was trying to communicate with the two Japanese girls at the desk. "Tse rum is on tse zecond floor. Tsis iz tse key."

"Rum?" the Japanese girls asked in confusion.

"Man, I'm just the temp help here," the woman explained wearily to Tina after the other guests had gone. "But you're in luck. A family suite has just come free. Kids came down with chicken pox, so the family left early. Otherwise, the only other option would've been the dormitory. It's a little cheaper but isn't handicap accessible. Along with the membership fee, that'll be seventy euros."

"We'll take the suite," Tina replied as she set several crumpled bills on the counter.

For some reason, it felt as if she were checking into a by-the-hour motel. But the woman didn't even glance at them. In any case, she didn't look as if she'd had one calm moment to watch TV or read the newspaper in the last twenty-four hours.

"Just fill this out." She pushed a form across to Tina, who neatly filled it out with a false address for the Tom family from Neuburg. Marvelous, that was done, although the meagre remainder of their cash worried her a little. However, if everything went smoothly, they would reach Oskar's house the following day.

~

They took long showers and got dressed, and because there wasn't much to do in their room and Oskar insisted that he didn't want to go to bed yet, they went down to the TV room. A group of young Brits was lounging around in there, drinking beer and loudly discussing where they could stay for the least amount of money the following night. On the TV, a rerun of an old detective show was running, but nobody was paying any attention to it. Several of the guests were sitting in a row on the couch, all studying their phone screens. A large American family was examining a map of Würzburg, from which the children were reading loudly and being praised for it. A couple dressed in identical Sydney sweatshirts was playing cards in the corner of the room.

No one paid attention to Tina and her companions as they entered the room, and nobody cared when Tina changed the TV channel and attempted to find a news program. There. Susi appeared on the screen once more. Paul had been right. She *had* put on a lot of weight, which Tina hadn't noticed that afternoon because the camera had focused only on her face. Had this been caused by stress? Since the breakup of Susi's second marriage, nothing in the relationship category had happened for her, as Tina now recalled. This was why she had thrown herself headfirst into her work. Or was her job the reason Susi had no time or patience for another relationship? Didn't matter. Tina dragged Markus along with her, and the three of them sat down close together, right in front of the TV, so they could hear everything while also blocking the screen from the other guests.

"The police are doing everything in their power to locate the abducted Oskar Krauss," Susi was in the process of explaining to the group of assembled journalists and camera crew. It looked like she was giving a press conference. *"I am certain that Mr. Krauss is still alive and that he hasn't been injured."*

A murmur rippled through the viewers. As the cameras flashed, someone called out, *"What makes you so sure of that, Inspector?"* Susi ignored the interruption and turned toward someone who wasn't visible on the screen.

"Of course she's sure," Tina whispered. "She knows us. She celebrated New Year's with us twenty-five years ago and went on vacation with us and borrowed my clothes. She knows we wouldn't hurt a fly."

"Man, she's a right Karen, isn't she?" Markus shook his head. "I'm still glad that I decided to pursue you back then and not Susi."

"As if you'd ever—"

"You've got to be kidding," Oskar interrupted. "Now they're dragging Volker into this!"

Indeed, Susi was gently leading a man to the microphone, as if she were taking him to identify a marsh corpse. *"Mr. Volker Benecke is the son-in-law of the kidnapped Oskar Krauss,"* she informed the journalists. *"He is now going to make an appeal to the kidnappers."*

Son-in-law Volker was wearing what looked like pajamas and had obviously stopped shaving at some point around Easter. He squinted like a confused and startled nocturnal animal that had been dragged into the light of day. A woman about ten years younger than Tina was clinging to his arm. She possessed several chins, and her hair had wild highlights. Like Volker, she had seen better days. Oskar's daughter?

"Yikes, Angela looks awful." Oskar shook his head.

Volker Benecke cleared his throat at least three times and pulled a crumpled piece of paper out of his pocket. *"To the kidnappers,"* he started to read haltingly. *"I implore you to release my father-in-law. Oskar Krauss has a serious heart condition. He is a frail man with advanced dementia. He has no idea what he is doing or where he is, and he must be terrified right now. He has run away multiple times and has incontinence problems, and he belongs in a care home, so that he can spend his final days surrounded by his loved ones and medical professionals."* Volker Benecke exhaled, exhausted; reading presumably stressed him out.

"We beg you to bring our poor, sick, old daddy back. Let his family and not his abductors be the last thing he sees in this life. Don't hurt him. In his condition, he no longer understands what is happening to him." A tear rolled down Volker Benecke's large-pored cheek, and he wiped it away with the sleeve of his odd leisure suit.

Another murmur rippled through the crowd, and then stunned silence spread throughout the room.

"That conniving, lying bastard!" Oskar cursed so loudly that even the British travelers stopped making noise for a moment and looked across at them with interest.

"Yes, *bastard*! Ten-hut!" one of them called back enthusiastically as he raised his glass in an unsteady salute. His comrades laughed.

"He's standing there in his baggy getup and lying through his teeth," Oskar thundered. "Heart condition. Bed wetting. Dementia. Final days!" Oskar was agitated. Tina hadn't seen him like that before.

"Oskar, I'm sor—"

"And as for the last thing I want to see on this earth, it is guaranteed not you, you bonehead!" Oskar shook his fist threateningly at the TV. "You have to help me. Help me avenge this insult. I have tolerated everything from Volker long enough, for my daughter's sake. But enough is enough. This much idiocy must be punished." In anger, he slammed his fist onto the plastic table sitting next to him, and as he did so, he swept an informational brochure for the city of Würzburg onto the floor.

"Absolutely, Oskar. Of course we'll help you. What do you have in mind?" Markus exuded decisiveness. And even Tina couldn't deny a certain degree of euphoria. This lame brain in a leisure suit had earned a taking down. What was that idiot thinking? Oskar was such a clever old man. How could anyone miss that about him?

"I don't know yet. Something that will make him insanely angry. Something that will make him see what it feels like to be labeled as mentally incompetent. Something like . . ." Oskar struggled to find the words but couldn't.

Markus glanced around the hostel's TV room and studied the loud young men with their beer bottles; the Japanese travelers, who were streaming into the room in growing numbers; and the large American family, which had by now covered the entire table as well as the floor around them with cards and travel guides and brochures and peanut butter sandwiches and soft drink cans. Suddenly, a devious little smile appeared on his face. "I have an idea," he said. "Oskar, what is your son-in-law's address?"

Oskar told him. Markus nodded, stood up, and walked over to a computer in the corner of the room that was available for hostel guest use. He quickly typed something up and then printed off a stack of pages.

"Here," he said, giving Tina and Oskar a conspiratorial wink. "Let's pass these out to our international friends." He pressed half of his stack into Tina's hands.

"What's this?"

"Read it. Fortunately, my English isn't completely rusty."

Tina started to read. Her eyes grew wide.

> Free lodging at Germany's newest youth hostel!
>
> Our newly opened hostel in Ingolstadt is offering you three free nights plus breakfast!
>
> Enjoy your stay in our beautifully renovated modern facilities and take in the sights and treasures of Ingolstadt, the secret jewel in the crown of Germany's cities!

This offer is only valid for the first hundred guests who hand in this voucher.

We look forward to seeing you!

Volker and Angela Benecke, hostel managers

Bergstrasse 14

Ingolstadt

"Markus, you are my hero." Tina stood up, kissed her husband, and started to hand out the flyers.

15

At 9:00 a.m., Tina woke up to the sound of loud laughter from the street below. She squinted in confusion and glanced around. There was a van Gogh print on the wall, and she heard an unknown voice outside shout, "Get your backpack!" With that, she remembered that they had spent the night in a youth hostel. That wasn't the only strange thing. She sensed Markus's eyes on her and turned over.

"How long have you been awake?" she asked, astonished.

He normally squeezed out every bit of sleep he could and engaged in an equally bitter and hopeless battle against his alarm clock on a daily basis. This struggle didn't end until one final angry whack was given to the clock, which then fell silent. Markus would haul himself out of bed at this point, grumpy as a bear disturbed from its hibernation.

"For quite a while. I couldn't fall back asleep, because my mind wouldn't calm down."

Tina didn't respond.

"Tina, I . . . Are you mad at me? Because I screwed everything up. I'm so terribly sorry. I wish I could turn back time, honestly."

"I don't," Tina heard herself reply to her own surprise. "I wouldn't want to do that. I'm glad that we're where we are right now."

"Really? I thought you hated me because I'd messed up our lives."

Sitting up in bed, Tina reached for his hand. "No, you haven't. Of course, I still don't know what will happen to us, but the last two days have been the best I've had in ages. You freed me from an unbelievably dull job, which I shuffled off to every day as if I were going to my execution. I never would've had the courage to just quit. If you hadn't held up the gas station, the two of us would've spent the rest of our days rotting away at our miserable jobs, assuming they didn't force us out eventually due to advanced age. We never would've met Oskar, and Oskar would've already ended up at that awful Luisenhaus nursing home, and nobody would've ever seen what a fantastic person he is. No, Markus, I'm not mad at you. I'm grateful. It's as if . . ." She fell silent for a moment. "It's as if you suddenly woke up from a coma," she said, trying to make him understand. "As if the true Markus from years ago unexpectedly crept out of the cocoon he'd been snoozing in for years."

Markus smiled at her. "Just with less hair."

Tina gently touched his receding hairline. "In exchange, you've developed different qualities over the years. And I'm not exactly Sweet Sixteen anymore, but that doesn't matter either. We have each other and our Paul. We aren't one of those couples who are just staying together for convenience's sake, nor are we like that dreadful Katie and her weird husband at the wedding."

"But she was hot!"

"What did you say?"

"If you like battleaxes in veiled hats, that is," Markus quickly added.

"Well, I think you missed your chance with her. And with the cute salesclerk too." Tina gave him a slight slap. "I can't tell you how excited I am about going to the North Sea," she continued, lacing her fingers behind her head and staring at the ceiling. "Maybe we could take the ferry across to Föhr again and find that little harbor restaurant we liked so much the last time we were there. After we've dropped Oskar off, that is."

"And then we could sit on the beach, and I can play for you on my air guitar." Markus pretended like he was practicing for his solo performance. "Sorry I don't have the real one with me."

"Air guitar will do just fine."

"What?!" Markus threw a pillow at her head. "Are you saying that you've never liked my guitar playing?"

"After a few bottles of wine, it was quite bearable."

"Aha! I can't believe it. Well, in that case, I'll need to impress you with some of the other qualities I've picked up over the years. How does that sound?" And with that, he pulled her up against him.

~

When they climbed into the Jeep two hours later, freshly showered and ready to leave, it occurred to Tina that the hostel looked strangely abandoned. This morning, instead of the woman from the previous evening, an eager-looking blond man with glasses was working at the front desk. Tina decided to steer clear of him so she could avoid answering any awkward questions.

"So," Markus said once all the car doors were shut. "Everyone on board? Now we'll drive all the way, and in about seven hours, we should get there."

A buzz came from the stolen cell phone. Oskar looked at it. "Look at this," he said. "The guy keeps getting messages and spicy photos from someone saved as SweetTart1990. She keeps sending one text after the other."

"How could anyone want to be with a man like that?" Tina asked. "There was nothing appealing about him at all."

"I don't think it's his personality she's after. Listen to this: Snugglebunny, why aren't you answering? We were going to go shopping, remember? I yearn for you. Smack!" Oskar read.

"Snugglebunny? That's hysterical!" Markus hit the steering wheel for emphasis.

"Write her back." Oskar handed Tina the phone. "My fingers are too awkward for all that typing, but I'd be glad to dictate the message."

"Okay, shoot."

"Sweet Tart—this is Snugglebunny's wife. Leave my husband alone and put on some clothes! P.S. I hope you get cavities from your stupid nickname!"

Hilarious. Tina hit the send button. After that, silence reigned. She decided to kill time by calling Fashion World again to fill Marion in on the newest developments. This time, she got lucky; Marion answered the phone.

"Fashion World, everything for the woman. My name is Ms. Walter. How can I help you?" Marion asked with the enthusiasm of a burned-out light bulb.

"I would like to order thirty corduroy blazers in chartreuse in size 3X," Tina said, picturing Marion's face with almost hysterical delight. "They're so snazzy."

"Wha—" Marion gasped. "Tina? Is that you?"

"Yes, of course it's me. Do you honestly think there's a single mentally competent person on the face of the planet who would order thirty of those ugly things?" Tina burst out laughing.

"Man, Tina! And you actually sound happy. That's insane! Where are you? Have you heard how everyone's tearing their hair out to find you?" Marion lowered her voice. "Müller's been telling people that you almost beat her up when she asked about borrowing a pen from you and that she wasn't the least bit surprised that you've turned out to be a psychopath."

"If only I had beaten her up back then," Tina said.

"What?"

"Just kidding. I threw a pen at her, that much is true. But only because she was too lazy to stand up and walk over to my desk. The pen bounced off her backside anyway. It was as if I had thrown a match at a beach ball. She's lying. But it doesn't really matter. I'm just calling to tell you goodbye, because I won't be coming back to Fashion World."

"Ever?" Marion's voice sounded panic stricken. "What do you mean? You can't just abandon me to this crappy place and all the whining customers!"

"Then don't stay there. Life is much too short."

"What are you planning? Where are you going?"

"I'm not completely sure, but even if I did know, I couldn't tell you, otherwise the police could interrogate you about us. All I do know is that I won't ever come back to Fashion World."

"I get it." Marion fell silent, obviously impressed. She then continued, her tone truly pleading. "Tina, say—could you kidnap me too? Like the old grandpa? Please, please get me out of here! I mean, I don't have it in me to quit, but if you kidnapped me, that would count as an act of God, so to speak, and I wouldn't have to work here anymore. I can't stand it. They just showed us the new fall catalog, and it takes ugliness to a whole new level. There's even a carrot-orange full-body angora jumpsuit with pom-poms, available up to 4X—"

"Marion, quit. Don't put it off. I'll be back in touch, okay?"

"Kidnap me, Tina! Please! Excellent, the corduroy blazer in chartreuse, our most popular piece, just so you know. Anything else?"

The boss. No doubt she was standing behind Marion and staring over her shoulder with her beady eyes.

"No, thank you very much, Ms. Walter." Tina hung up.

"Marion wants us to abduct her," she told Markus.

"Gladly!" Oskar said. "I always enjoy female companionship."

"Marion is married. And besides, she's much too young for you, Oskar. You aren't anyone's Snugglebunny, right?"

All three of them laughed, and Tina thought this was a good opportunity to find out more about Oskar's mysterious love life.

"Elise, the woman you mentioned the other day," she began. "Did you ever try to figure out where she's living now? Or is she already . . . ?"

"No, I don't think so. She was fifteen years younger than me," Oskar said. "But regardless, why would I have done that? She chose someone else all those years ago . . ." He stopped talking. A semi from France was now passing them, and Oskar stared hard at the dancing wheel of Camembert on its side.

"Who did she choose?" Tina pressed.

"She chose my best friend, if you must know. He helped things along a little, of course. He brainwashed her with all his compliments and promises. It also didn't hurt that he was stinking rich."

"How horrible!" Tina felt outraged. "And you put up with that?"

"What was I supposed to do? Love can't be forced. Maybe she's been happy with him. I have no idea. And I don't want to know either." Oskar continued to stare stubbornly out the window.

"What's her full name?" Tina asked. She had an idea and pulled out the stolen phone.

"Her name was Elise Weigel, but she probably took his last name, which would make her Elise Bartenstock."

Bartenstock. Fortunately, that name was unusual enough that it wouldn't produce hundreds of hits. Tina typed the name into the search page, and . . .

"Bingo!" she said. "An Elise Bartenstock lives in Husum. Could that be her?"

"Yes, I can't believe it! That has to be her . . . They actually still live in Husum." Oskar was astounded.

"I'm going to call her," Tina decided, instantly hitting the number that had appeared in her search.

"What?! What are you going to say to her? Don't you dare tell her anything about me!" Oskar twisted around in his seat and gripped the headrest.

"Bartenstock residence," a woman's voice quickly answered. She sounded too young to be a woman over seventy. A daughter? Or granddaughter?

"I would like to speak with Elise Bartenstock."

A brief suspicious silence. "My mother isn't here. May I take a message?"

"I . . . am an acquaintance of hers." Tina floundered for an explanation. She almost hung up, but she needed to get one more bit of information. "Is your father available?" she ventured.

The woman on the other end didn't answer for a few seconds. "What do you want? Who is this? My father has been dead for over a decade. Why do you want to speak with my mother?"

"I . . . please accept my apologies," Tina mumbled before ending the call as fast as she could.

Oskar was staring at her as if spellbound. "Well?"

"She wasn't there, but neither was her husband. He passed away over ten years ago."

"So, Helmut has kicked the bucket? Ha, fate has a sense of humor sometimes!"

"Come on now, Oskar." Markus shook his head.

"Sorry, that was in bad taste. But sometimes life really does have its own sense of humor, doesn't it? Anyway, considering that Helmut was a chain-smoker whose hero was the Marlboro Man, this isn't all that surprising."

"Oskar, she lives in Husum," Tina said slowly. "Markus, are you thinking what I'm thinking?"

"Definitely. I think we should stop by. What do you think, Oskar? Just to say hi as we're passing through?"

Oskar didn't reply. He was concentrating on the seam of his new T-shirt.

"Oskar?" Tina nudged him. For the first time since she had met him, he seemed to be at a loss for words.

"Maybe." His voice was little more than a whisper.

"Not maybe—we're definitely doing this." Tina was about to give a small discourse on old, never-fading love, when she noticed a small tear glittering in Oskar's eye. With that, she fully dismissed his claim that Elise no longer mattered to him.

~

"Bathroom stop," she said a few hours later. They had already covered over half the distance, but it was still at least two or three hours to Husum, and Tina needed to stretch her legs.

“I’d rather get off the autobahn for that.” Markus changed lanes. “There are too many people at the rest areas right along the road. Somebody’d be bound to recognize us. We can’t risk that so close to our destination.”

Oskar nodded. “Markus would’ve made an excellent conniving crook in my day. It’s a shame you didn’t pop up in my life when I was younger. You and I would’ve had a grand time!”

“Just like we are now.” Markus exchanged a conspiratorial smile with the old man before taking the next exit. They drove a short way through the flat landscape, which looked so different from the area around Ingolstadt. Tina could’ve sworn that the sky up here was bluer and the air fresher. A poster advertising the Walsrode World Bird Park sported pink flamingos standing in a row along a lakeshore like parked cars.

“Pull over anywhere you think I can find a bathroom and coffee,” Tina said.

“Hoffmann’s Alternative Organic Farm,” Markus read off a roadside sign. “Homemade bread, coffee, and pastries. Does that work?”

Tina nodded. “It does for me, as long as I don’t have to pee in some composting outhouse.”

“Eco farmers should suit our needs,” Oskar cut in. “The more alternative, the better. They don’t tend to be on the best of terms with the meddlesome government, and they see themselves as guerilla fighters in aprons, armed with pitchforks. They’d be more likely to pelt the cops with pasture-raised eggs than to hand us over to them. Off we go.”

~

In reality, they were welcomed into a spacious kitchen by a cheerful woman with long hair who was wearing brightly colored rubber boots and a billowing caftan. Several children were swarming across the farmyard. A couple of chickens darted around, while a cat dozed in the sun.

Under a large pear tree in a meadow, an improvised café had been set up with folding tables and mismatched chairs.

"Perfect." Tina smiled at the woman.

"Would you like to try a sample? The crumb cake is fresh and was made with spelt flour," she told them as she handed them little pieces of cake. "It's delicious, try it!" She looked behind her. "Leo, do we still have any apple cider?" she called to her husband, who was kneeling next to a tractor, busy repairing something. A radio sitting beside him played music.

"There should be enough," he replied without looking up. His wife took their orders and returned to the kitchen.

Tina turned her face toward the sun and listened to the music from the radio, the chirping of the birds, and the buzzing of the bees. Kicking off her shoes, she took a deep breath. "This is paradise. Markus, why can't we live like this too?" He didn't answer. "Markus?"

"Psst, Tina, listen. The news is coming on."

"Up next, curiosities from across the country. Today's story comes from Ingolstadt," a lively man's voice announced.

Ingolstadt? Tina's eyes widened, and she pricked up her ears.

"This morning, there was a mass incident in Ingolstadt involving twenty-two young Japanese travelers, fourteen Brits, ten Americans, and smaller numbers of individuals from other nations. This group stormed the home of an unsuspecting Ingolstadt couple, where they demanded free lodging and breakfast. Overwhelmed, the husband couldn't defend himself and was inadvertently locked into his own pantry, while the young globe-trotters checked out his house and made themselves at home. They had been given advertising flyers that alleged that this was the location of a newly opened youth hostel. The reason for this misunderstanding is still unclear. However, what we do know is that neighbors eventually called the police to file a disturbing-the-peace complaint. The homeowner is apparently suffering from a nervous breakdown. They say he hurled jelly jars from the pantry at the police, thinking they were more tourists. The homeowner was taken to a nearby psychological clinic by an ambulance, at the sight of which he started

to shout and rave. The entire incident was filmed and has gone viral online. Yes, dear listeners, things like this do happen in real life, so be sure to lock your doors and don't open up for strangers. First and foremost, though, stay cool, because now it's time for the weather. It's going to stay sunny, sunny, sunny, with highs in the nineties. And with that in mind, here comes the 1983 hit 'Sunshine Reggae' from Laid Back . . ."

As the music started, Tina thought that Oskar was going to choke to death, because he swallowed a whole mouthful of cake. But then she realized to her relief that he was just shaking with laughter. "Amazing!" he cackled. "What an absolute treat! Now my life is complete!"

"Isn't it?" the farmwife called out to them with pride. "Such a treat, I always say. And organic too!"

16

Elise's house was a multistory white mansion with large windows. It was located on a quiet side street in Husum, surrounded by green space. The upper windows probably had a glorious sea view. Tina would've given her left hand to live in such an amazing home. Well, maybe not her entire hand, but at least one or two fingers. Obviously, Elise had won the lottery when it came to Oskar's former friend. Some people really did have all the luck.

They parked the Jeep on the street, although parking was supposedly only for residents. One ticket more or less wouldn't make a difference. The business guy's liability insurance might cover it anyway. Or his attorney would fight it tooth and nail.

"Now what?" Oskar asked. "What do you have in mind? Do you want to drag me to the door and leave me in front of it while you ring the bell and run away?"

"Of course not. We'll stay with you. And we'll just say . . ." Tina hesitated. Well, what, actually?

"What if she slams the door? Or if she says, *We don't give handouts. Take the old man away!*" Oskar was now blowing things a little out of proportion.

"But she'll recognize you!" Markus raised an eyebrow, clearly entertained.

"Really? Are you so sure? The last time she saw me, I was fifty years younger. Fifty! You're probably not even that old yet. I still had hair on my head and none in my ears. My pants sat loose around my hips and never rode up to my armpits for some strange reason. And when I fell asleep, no nurse came running to see if I was still breathing!"

"We'll see." Tina got out of the car. "Worst case, she'll tell us to get lost. And that'll be it."

Oskar muttered something, pulled a little comb out of his pocket, and carefully combed the white wreath of hair on his head. "What?" he snapped at Tina, when he caught her watching him.

"I'm just amazed, Oskar. Not all that long ago, you said that beauty creeps inside with age." Tina bit her lip to keep from laughing.

"That only goes for other people. I personally get sexier the older I get." He paused for effect. "Hotter with every candle on the cake."

Tina grasped his arm. "You certainly do. Come on, let's get this behind us."

The blond woman who opened the door was younger than Tina, or at least looked like it. She was wearing an expensive blue suit, and her hair was pinned up in a style that never would have stayed so perfectly in place on Tina but would have uncoiled wildly within seconds.

"Can I help you?" the woman asked coolly as she studied them.

Tina was glad that she had at least used the businessman's money to get a new summer dress, although she instantly sensed that women like this wouldn't touch such a dress with a ten-foot pole.

"We would like to speak with Mrs. Elise Bartenstock," Markus said. "It won't take long."

The woman didn't budge an inch. "Did you call earlier?"

"Yes, that was me," Tina stuttered. Looking back, it struck her that what she had done had been a little intrusive. Why hadn't she just explained on the phone what she wanted? "We would really like to speak with your mother."

"Listen, who are you? You haven't even told me your names." The blond woman took a minuscule step back into the cool darkness of her elegant home. "My mother is napping, and I won't just wake her up because some people"—the woman drew out the word in an especially condescending way—"have showed up and want to talk to her."

She's annoyed with us, Tina thought. *She's about to shut the door.* She hadn't even considered the possibility that they wouldn't be allowed to see Elise.

With that, Oskar suddenly moved forward. He had gotten up from his wheelchair and now stood a little unsteadily in front of the young woman, an unwavering smile on his face.

"Just tell her that Blaze is at the door," he said. "And these two are Ingolstadt's own Bonnie and Clyde."

"Excuse me? Who?" Apparently, Oskar had finally managed to rattle the cool blonde.

"Blaze. She'll know what that means."

"Who's there?" a woman's voice called down from upstairs. "Is it for me?"

"It's . . ." The blond woman paused but decided to at least pass the message on to her mother. "There is an old man here, who says that his name is Blaze and that you know him. And then there's a Bonnie and . . . I mean, another man and woman with him."

No sound came from the stairs.

"Blaze?" Tina shot Oskar a curious glance.

"My hair." He tapped at his bald pate. "My hair used to be reddish blond. *Everywhere.* It helped me spark more than one fire over the years, and Elise—"

"Obviously, you're mistaken. My mother doesn't seem to know you," the blond woman quickly interjected. She was about to close the door on them when the voice from the stairs called out. Incredulous, shocked, but also joyful.

"Blaze? Did you say Blaze? That's impossible!"

They heard footsteps running down the steps with astounding agility. And then she materialized at the door—Oskar's Elise. She looked like an older version of her daughter, although she lacked the uppity air the younger woman had perfected. Elise was composed solely of laugh lines and high spirits. "Blaze?" she cried. "Oskar, is it really you?"

"In all my youthfulness," Oskar said modestly as he held on to Markus. "The blaze up on my head might have gone out, but the one in here"—he tapped his chest—"still burns strong."

"Oskar! It's you!" And with that, the old woman hugged him so enthusiastically that Tina braced him from behind him to keep him from toppling over.

~

Before long, Elise's daughter was pouring tea for Tina and Markus from a fancy porcelain teapot, passing around rock sugar and a pretty cream pitcher and silver spoons. Tina had never drunk tea in such a genteel manner; she hadn't had the time for it. She typically tossed a tea bag into a mug, poured hot water over it, squeezed the bag out a few minutes later, and then dropped it as a crumpled mass into the sink to dry.

"Thank you." Tina took one of the elegant butter cookies the daughter offered them on a silver platter.

"Enjoy," the young woman said. "We order them from a historic bakery in Lübeck. By the way, my name is Viktoria. Please pardon my rather cool welcome, but you wouldn't believe how many of my father's so-called friends have turned up here in recent years wanting to talk to my mother. Because he allegedly still owes them money or once promised them something. All just beggars. You can't be too cautious around people like that."

"That's okay," Tina said right away. "We understand." *We're well acquainted with debt,* she almost added.

Laughter drifted over from the neighboring room. Elise was giving Oskar a tour of the house, which was obviously a source of amusement for both of them.

"I haven't seen my mother this happy in a long time," Victoria remarked, loosening up more and more with each passing minute.

"Oskar, hands off, you rascal!" they heard from the adjacent room, closely followed by Oskar's rumbling laughter. Something fell to the floor with a clatter.

Markus and Tina exchanged a look. What in the world was Oskar up to?

"That was just the umbrella stand," he shouted, as if he could read their thoughts.

"All righty." Tina cleared her throat and searched for an innocuous topic for conversation. "Your mother probably hasn't had much to laugh about the past ten years. I'm sure her husband's death saddened her."

To her astonishment, Viktoria waved this off. "No, not really. You see, my parents' marriage was . . ." She took a tiny sip of her tea. "My father often left my mother on her own, especially in his final years. There were also—" She broke off, apparently realizing that she was on the verge of divulging family secrets. But Tina could guess what Viktoria had been about to say. *There were other women.* The few photos of Elise's husband sitting around her exquisitely decorated living room had conveyed a certain impression. A bon vivant. Handsome, expensively dressed, with a hungry look in his eyes. A ladies' man.

"It wasn't a particularly happy marriage?" Tina wagered a guess.

"No, I don't think so," Viktoria admitted as she set down her cup. "That's why I'm glad that her . . . Blaze wanted to stop by."

The door opened, and Elise and Oskar entered. He reached for one of the framed photographs and studied it. "Is that old Inge in this picture? Was this at your wedding? What was she wearing? Looks like a carpet."

"Leave poor Inge alone." Elise laughed and took the photo away from him. "She was always a nice friend. And some women can't rock just anything, but that's okay, as long as they're comfortable."

"And some men can strip down naked and still can't rock it. But that's okay, as long as they're comfortable," Oskar replied. Tina, Markus, and Elise burst out laughing. After a moment of shocked silence, Viktoria did too. The ice was finally broken.

"What did you end up doing with the ambulance?" Elise asked after they had calmed down again.

Tina spilled a few drops of tea in her surprise. "You know about that?" Had Oskar told her everything?

"Of course! I've been following your thrilling hunt on television. Nothing exciting happens around here, except whenever a seagull gets caught in the chimney. I just didn't know that the ominously vulnerable Mr. Krauss was Blaze. The news reports would have had us believe that the man was practically at death's door."

"Which he isn't," Oskar replied. "And we got rid of that vehicle."

"But where are you going?" Elise wanted to know. "You could stay here for a while, if you like."

"That's awfully nice of you, darling, but there's something we need to take care of. We want to get to my old house in Wobbenbüll."

"The house at Landweg 14? You still own it?" Elise looked startled. "Why didn't you ever sell it?"

"Because I always knew that I would come back someday. This is where everything that ever mattered to me is."

A brief silence ensued, during which a tender flush spread across Elise's face. Tina could see it, plain as day.

"More tea, anyone?" Viktoria finally said and poured some for Oskar before he could respond. Tina leaned back and discreetly studied her surroundings. As far as she was concerned, she wouldn't mind spending a few days here. Everything was top notch. Money—and a lot of it—was evident everywhere she looked. Oskar hadn't exaggerated in his description of Helmut's wealth. However, despite the house on the sea, the cashmere cardigans, and the silver flatware, Elise had clearly been unhappy in her marriage. Had she ever regretted her decision? Tina looked at the old woman, who no longer struck her as all that old. Her posture was straight and tall, and she didn't seem frail in the slightest. She was neatly groomed and quite cheerful.

Viktoria had opened the French doors out onto the terrace, and a fresh sea breeze swept in. At that moment, almost everything was exactly as Tina had imagined it on that cursed lunch break a few days ago. The only difference was that she wasn't in Italy but in Husum. The old Tina and her old life felt strangely surreal, as if they were somehow part of a parallel universe.

"We should be hitting the road," Oskar said. "We still have a few things to take care of."

"In that case, give me your number, and I'll give you mine. Maybe we could meet up again soon." There was a pleading note in Elise's voice. She pulled an iPhone out of her pocket and waited.

"Wow, Elise! Aren't you modern?" Oskar pointed at her phone. "Do you take lots of selfies on that thing? Or photos of your food?"

"Sometimes. Why not?"

"In a thousand years, aliens will see our photos and think that we spent all our time in restaurants, taking pictures of our lunch."

"I couldn't care less about the aliens. You can also follow me on Instagram," Elise calmly fired back. "I'm under Elise's Tea Garden, where I give reviews of various kinds of tea. I already have over four hundred fifty followers."

"And now you have one more."

She smiled.

~

"Elise . . . she was always beautiful." Oskar was bubbling over with enthusiasm as they set off for Wobbenbüll. "But I never would've thought she'd still look so good. What did you think of her?"

"She's great," Markus said. "Her house was also pretty fabulous."

Oskar gave a disdainful sniff. "A golden cage. Helmut locked her up in there, and then he amused himself with other women."

So Tina had been right, after all. She sat up straight so she could see herself in the rearview mirror and tried to re-create Viktoria's hairstyle with just her hands. It was pointless. Her hair started to slip through her fingers right away.

"Elise deserved something better in her life," Oskar insisted. "She—"

"—deserved you," Markus finished his sentence. "That's obvious. But you might see her again and then—oh, where do I need to turn?"

He leaned forward and squinted so he could read the signs at the intersection.

"Left, down that little road," Oskar said without looking up. "I know this area like the back of my hand."

They drove past thatched red cottages. On their left, a field of grain waved in the wind, and far back on the horizon stood a lighthouse.

"It's beautiful here," Tina said. "Markus, drive a little slower. We don't have to speed to get there."

"I'm not speeding." Markus whipped around the next turn and promptly slammed on the brakes. A patrol car was driving right in front of them, and Markus had almost rear-ended it. "Shit!" he hissed.

The officer pulled over and motioned for them to do the same. A mustached officer with hair short in the front and long in the back climbed energetically out of his vehicle and strode toward them, a serious look on his face.

"Vehicle registration and driver's license, please," he barked. "Do you know what the speed limit is along here?"

"Uhh . . ." Markus nervously clenched his jaw. "Well, I think . . . this is a county road, right? Then, maybe sixty-five?"

"The speed limit is fifty," the officer growled as he held out his hand for the papers.

Tina couldn't believe it. She just couldn't believe it! Why in the world did this overzealous local cop have to cross their path just now? Why did Markus have to speed all the time?

"Let's first get the registration papers," Markus muttered as he fished something out of the glove compartment. "This is . . . a rental." He cleared his throat. "And where did I stick my license? Just a sec . . ." He was holding his license but couldn't bring himself to hand it over to the officer. He peered desperately at Tina in the rearview mirror, then across at Oskar, then at the officer, who had stepped in front of the Jeep and was giving the license plate number to someone over the radio. The expression on the officer's face suddenly changed. He looked alert now, practically ecstatic. He stared hard at Markus, like a snake at a rabbit.

"This car has been reported stolen. Please get out of the vehicle."

"Listen . . ." Markus started to say. "We borrowed the car from a friend, who's the manager at . . . Well, I can't seem to remember the name of the company. Anyway, he rented this car from some place, but I don't know its name either . . . Maybe . . ." Whatever else he was trying to say came out as a strangled gurgle. At this point, the officer barked a short "Get out!" as he took Markus's license and studied it.

Maybe he didn't know who they were. *God, please don't let him know who we are!* Tina prayed. *I gave that pastor half of our stolen money, and we picked up those two young hitchhikers. How could it all be over, so close to our destination?*

"Well, well, this just gets better and better," the officer rejoiced. Tina could have sworn that he was drooling at the fact that this lame evening stuck on a country road had finally brought him a score.

"I need backup, right now!" he yelled into his radio. "Stolen car and the suspects from that big manhunt in Bavaria in custody." He looked inside the Jeep. "The kidnapping victim is still alive. Urgently need an ambulance." The officer now raised his voice even louder. "Mr. Krauss, can you hear me? Medical assistance is on the way!"

"I'm not deaf, you know!" Oskar rumbled, but Tina could tell that he wasn't laughing anymore. This was it—the end. And this time, they didn't have any runaway teens who could get them off the hook. Her eyes began to tear up.

"Oskar, we—" she started, but the officer interrupted her.

"Please step out of the vehicle. And hands behind your back."

This village cop had actually pulled out handcuffs! This was bound to be the high point of his career. Tina closed her eyes for a moment. She had escaped the yoke of idiocy at Fashion World only to be waylaid out in the boondocks by some ambitious village sheriff with a mullet, while two crows circled overhead like vultures. Oskar was right. Life truly did have its own sense of humor. In the distance, Tina now heard a howling police siren, which seemed to be greeting her, mocking her, like an old friend.

17

The village officer's backup looked like his twin brother, just in blond, and at the sight of Tina and Markus, he got the same eager, greedy look around his mouth. Tina thus concluded that nothing of any significance had happened here since the moon landing, and that she and Markus offered an attraction that would be hard to top. In fact, a veritable fair-like atmosphere dominated the precinct to which they took Tina and Markus. People were standing around everywhere, whispering and laughing and staring at them.

Whether she wanted to or not, Tina felt ashamed and could feel her face blushing dark red. The more aware she became of this, the more the flush spread from her neckline to her ears. What a shitty, ignominious end for Ingolstadt's own Bonnie and Clyde!

She was taken into a small room that held a table and two chairs, as well as an abandoned cup of cold coffee. Obviously, the dearth of active criminals around here had, until just now, resulted in the playing of card games. A joker was lying face up on the table and seemed to be laughing at Tina.

Markus was led to the other side of the room, which was separated from Tina's by nothing but a tall filing shelf. *There isn't even a decent interrogation room here,* Tina thought. And for some reason, she found this especially humiliating.

A potted baobab tree was dying of dehydration on the windowsill. Maps and a poster of a lighthouse were hanging on the wall. On a small cabinet, a Happy 50th Birthday card promised that this was the point when life really got started. A soccer game on mute flickered from a TV mounted on the wall.

Tina craned her neck to catch a glimpse of Markus, but at that moment, the village cop cleared his throat and turned to face her with a satisfied grin.

"So," he said. "We finally caught you. Your days of flying high are over now."

As if we ever flew all that high, Tina thought grimly. However, she decided not to let herself get annoyed. "Where is Mr. Krauss?"

"You'd like to know that, wouldn't you?" the officer shot back smugly. "But you won't be finding that out, nor will you be able to do anything else to that poor old man. He's safe now. His relatives will be notified and will be coming to get him."

His relatives. Tina felt a lump form in her throat. Whatever she and Markus were going to face now—something she didn't wish to imagine in great detail—it was nothing compared to what poor Oskar would be facing. Back into the clutches of his greedy son-in-law, who was probably waiting for him with the mental-incompetence papers already signed. Back to the care home, where everything smelled like rubber, and apathetic or overworked nurses would push a heavily medicated Oskar into a glass conservatory, where he would doze away the twilight of his years sandwiched between artificial plants and other sedated home residents.

"I would like to speak to my son," Tina said. "And my attorney." As if she actually had the latter, but anyway. Keep bluffing. She had learned at least that much from Oskar.

"You can tell all that to my colleagues from Ingolstadt," the officer countered. "They're already on their way. They happened to be at a meeting in Hannover and should be here soon. Sometimes you just get lucky, right?"

Tina resisted the urge to hurl the old coffee sitting on the table in his face.

"Anyway." The officer cleared his throat again and looked at her sternly. "There are three officers sitting outside this room to make sure that you don't try to escape. So you should make yourself comfy in here until our fellow officers from Ingolstadt show up." His laugh sailed through the room and bounced off Tina.

"What if I need to go to the bathroom?" she asked in anger, lifting up her cuffed hands.

"Then just tell one of the officers." The cop strode authoritatively through the door. As soon as he left the room, she heard him shout something in a broad North German drawl. She couldn't make out what he said, but she knew what the ensuing laughter from the other men meant.

"Shit," Tina whispered. If only she could somehow talk to Markus. "Markus?" she called out quietly.

No reaction. "Markus?" she tried a little louder.

"Yes." A muted reply came from the other side of the barrier.

A thousand things she wanted to say to him shot through her mind. *Get us out of here. Do something, dammit.*

"I love you," she called out to him.

The officer at the glass door knocked on the pane and gave her a stern look.

"Love you too," Markus replied. And that was all they could say, because tears welled up in her eyes, and she didn't want him to know.

~

Two hours later, the small police precinct came to life. Doors slammed, and someone shouted, "They're here!" And as Tina, who defiantly had her back to the door, heard footsteps draw closer, she turned around and looked straight into a face she had once known almost as well as her own. Susi, her childhood friend. And yes, she was significantly larger than she had been before, but that offered little comfort to Tina at this point.

"I'm here to pick you up," Susi said slowly. "The police car is sitting at the door."

"Susi . . . I . . ." Tina didn't know how to start. "We didn't do anything to the old man. They told a bunch of lies about us. Okay, that thing at the gas station, that was a spur-of-the-moment thing. Markus only did that because he was so desperate, believe me. You know him. He couldn't hurt a fly. Me neither. We aren't criminals." Tina shook her cuffs in anger, and then suddenly on a whim, she repeated herself. "*None* of us are criminals. You aren't either."

Susi fell silent. Had she caught the reference? There was no way she could have forgotten.

"Susi? You know better than anyone what someone can do in desperation. Right, Susi? 1995, you remember. We—"

"I've come to pick you up," Susi interrupted.

How could she be so stubborn? She had to remember, after all that Tina had done for her back then. Tina couldn't believe it! "Really? They sent you out to the sticks, did they? Congratulations." Tina's voice dripped with disdain.

"No, quite the opposite. I asked them to let me take over this case."

"How nice for you." So she didn't have to make eye contact with Susi, Tina looked up at the TV. She did a double take.

"Turn it up," she told Susi.

"What?"

"The TV. You should turn it up. My son is on the screen."

Susi seemed just as startled as Tina was, and turned up the volume.

"A little more," Tina urged. "So Markus can listen in. He's over there. Markus? Can you hear?"

"—here, live in the studio, the son of the hunted couple, Tina and Markus Michel. Paul has agreed to answer a few questions for our viewers. Paul, did you ever pick up on anything that made you suspect that your parents were living a double life as criminals?"

"No, because my parents aren't leading double lives," Paul replied. Somebody in the studio laughed.

"But they've been on the run for several days and have more than a few felonies stacked up against them, including the kidnapping of a defenseless old man with a heart condition. Our viewers will find that less funny." No laughter this time.

"That might be," Paul conceded. *"But I know my parents would never, ever hurt an old man. My parents are really great people, and I . . ."* He took a deep breath as he searched for the right words. *"I'm proud of them, even if that isn't what your viewers want to hear."* The hint of an ironic and simultaneously guilty smile played about Paul's lips.

Tina's spirits started to rise. How had she and Markus ever deserved such a fantastic son?

"Did you hear that, Markus?" She shot Susi a triumphant look. She couldn't care less if Susi climbed the career ladder all the way up to the sky. Susi was perennially unlucky at love and had a lethargic goth daughter who smoked dope, as Tina had heard from Paul, who knew everything about everyone his age.

"Bravo, Paul!" Tina exclaimed. The screen went black. Susi had switched off the TV. She probably couldn't bear to see Tina's happy family.

"Let's go," she ordered Tina.

"Are you serious? You want to take us back to Ingolstadt today?"

Susi didn't reply. Was that supposed to be a yes? It was already getting dark. It would be long past midnight before they reached Ingolstadt. Maybe Susi was planning to speed the whole way back, using her blue lights. The thought of this almost made Tina laugh hysterically.

A police car was waiting for them at the door. A bored junior officer was sitting at the wheel.

"Get in, you two." Susi opened the back door, and for a moment, it looked like she wanted to press Tina's head down, like the cops in the movies always did.

Tina gave her a warning look, and Susi's hand jerked back.

At that moment, Tina realized that this was her last chance to speak with her old friend in private. "You still owe me," she whispered. "I thought you'd remember."

She had been the one who saved Susi's career. How could she ignore that so coldly? Years ago, right before her graduation from the police academy, duty-conscious Susi had had everything neatly planned out in both her professional and love lives for the next few decades. This was because a seemingly decent man had finally taken an interest in her. Heiner, the architect. A good catch, if you believed Susi's take on things, and absolutely high-karat husband material. They had joked about how Heiner and Markus would eventually have to get along, despite the fact that they couldn't stand each other. Markus had considered Heiner an arrogant jackass, and as for what Heiner thought about Markus, Susi had preferred to not say, but it was bound to have been less than flattering. And then one night, amazing Heiner had dropped potential wife Susi like a hot potato, because he had another girlfriend—a parallel one, so to speak, and for quite some time, as well. He had been "trying out" both of them to see which one suited him better, and Susi had obviously not passed the proverbial test, despite the fact she had already invested in his-and-her towels and matching toothbrush holders.

That night, Susi, bawling her eyes out, had emptied two bottles of wine with Tina, but had then insisted on driving herself home because the night bus wouldn't be coming through for at least another hour. Tina had had a bad feeling as she got into Susi's car, but she hadn't really wanted to wait an hour for the bus, either, especially since it was snowing and sleeting at the time.

When Susi tried to avoid hitting a rabbit on the dark road, she had rammed her car into a garden fence with the precision peculiar to drunk drivers. Besides the fence, she also cut a swath through a miniature landscape of garden gnomes and dwarf-size windmills. This wouldn't have been a major problem, in and of itself, if the furious homeowner hadn't called the police immediately.

Susi had begged Tina, pleaded with her, to tell the officer that she had been the one driving. If she didn't, Susi could kiss her career goodbye before she had even gotten started. And hadn't fate already run Susi through the ringer enough for one day?

As for Tina, she hadn't had a career that could be affected by something like this. She also didn't own a car, so a potential suspension of her driver's license wouldn't really matter.

Tina recalled that on that evening, in the face of the gnome massacre and the ever-thickening snow, she'd had just one wish: for the power to switch off the hysterically sobbing and moaning Susi. This was why she had agreed. What else could Tina have done? That's what friends were for, after all. Even if those friends contacted you only sporadically over the years as they worked their way up the career ladder. Even if something always seemed to pop up. Even if one day you realized you had hardly anything in common anymore except for the fact that you belonged to the same species.

Tina's license had been suspended for six months. Susi started with the police force, and soon after that, Tina had gotten pregnant.

"Susi?" Tina repeated, now imploringly. "You know what I'm talking about, right?"

"Get in." This was Susi's only response, and as Tina joined Markus in the back seat and saw his worried look, she wanted to start sobbing again. *But not in front of Susi,* she vowed.

~

After half an hour, Susi told the driver to pull over at a small rest stop, which was nothing more than a glorified outhouse with a bit of meadow and a shabby bench behind it. "I need to use the restroom," she told her colleague. The driver mumbled something. Susi turned toward Tina and Markus. "I assume you might need to go too?"

Tina gazed at her suspiciously. What was this? "No, I—" she started, but Susi interrupted her.

"You mentioned earlier that you have a weak bladder."

Tina stared at her, and Susi stared back, her expression inscrutable. A small, absurd hope flared up in Tina. Could it be that . . . ?

"Yes," she answered obediently. "I actually do. Badly."

Susi gave an almost imperceptible nod. "And you?" This was to Markus.

"Uhh . . ." Markus looked confused.

"Then the two of you come with me." Susi turned to the driver. "Kai, I'll take care of it." She got out of the vehicle. Markus was about to say something, but Tina gave him a gentle nudge. He shut his mouth again and looked at her, puzzled. Tina gave a little shrug and then walked into the stuffy log cabin with Markus and Susi on her heels. The latter still didn't say anything.

~

The inside of the women's restroom was dark and slippery. A long strip of crumpled toilet paper snaked along the floor like a trail to hell. It stank atrociously in there.

"Your last bathroom in freedom. Enjoy it," Susi said.

Tina spun around, intending to hurl her opinions of Susi at her old friend's head. But then she noticed Susi's expression. She was grinning, and that was remarkable for someone whose sense of humor tended to resemble that of a potted plant.

"Susi?" Tina asked slowly.

"Be quiet. I'm going to talk now. First, I'm going to take off your handcuffs. After all, you need to use the bathroom, and we German cops aren't monsters. Then you're going to overpower me and threaten me with my own service revolver. This one here. The safety's on."

"Wha—" Markus started to say, but Susi cut him off impatiently.

"And then you're going to cuff me"—Susi studied the space—"to that pipe back there. Stick something in my mouth first, so I can't call for help. Make sure it's clean, though, okay? Not that germy toilet paper. Throw the keys for the cuffs into some corner I can't reach and then hoof it into the woods behind the rest area, got it? Toss the gun into the bushes about ten yards into the trees. I have no desire to spend untold hours searching the entire forest for it. So, hurry up now! Kai isn't exactly the brightest bulb in the pack, but he won't wait out there forever. You should have about eight minutes as a head start."

Tina nodded automatically, her thoughts racing. This was their one and only chance to get away. But at the same time, it was the final step into full-blown criminality. Overpowering a police officer was a high-speed train straight into a life underground. It wasn't something they could ever talk their way out of if they got caught again—and the chances of that happening were high.

"Markus?" She looked at him. Their entire future together hung on that one word.

He gave a barely perceptible nod. "This is as good as it gets," he said. It sounded casual, but his voice trembled slightly.

"Okay." Tina turned to her friend. "Susi, I . . . Thank you . . ." She choked with excitement.

"Just do it!" Susi unlocked their cuffs. "Go!"

Markus was the first to shake off his momentary paralysis. He pulled Susi over the pipe and snapped the cuffs around her wrist. He then reached into his pocket and pulled out a handkerchief. "It's still clean," he insisted when he caught Susi's look.

"I hope so. Now get out of here. I can't take this stench for long."

"Susi, why are you doing this?" Tina asked before Markus could stuff the cloth in her mouth. "Because of back then?"

"In part. And because kidnapping carries a sentence of five years and armed robbery a minimum of three. If you have a good lawyer, it might be less, but I know you couldn't afford one. And you've already served your own fifteen years of incarceration at Fashion World." A hint of a smile flitted across Susi's face.

Tina gulped. "Susi . . . thank you. I'm really sorry that in recent years we haven't—"

"Just get out of here!" Susi interrupted. "Otherwise you'll be sorry for something else." And with that, she nodded at Markus, who gently stuck the handkerchief into her mouth and grabbed Tina's hand.

"Come on, let's go!"

Tina stumbled breathlessly behind Markus as thoughts tumbled through her head. All the excitement was making her feel sick and more than a little woozy.

"Down here," Markus urged, pushing her down a footpath that stretched from the restrooms to the woods.

Twigs left scratches across Tina's bare legs and face, and pine needles rained down into her hair. She twisted her ankle at some point, but fortunately the pain vanished after a few moments.

"Where are we going?" she panted as she tried to keep up with Markus. They couldn't hear a sound from the rest area.

"I don't know, just away from here. There's a road up there. Maybe someone will give us a ride." Markus didn't look around, just plowed straight through the underbrush. His now unbuttoned shirt fluttered behind him like a flag.

Tina eventually caught a glimpse of the lonely, pothole-ridden country lane that ran parallel to the copse they were in. At that moment, she realized that what she saw meant that their odds of being rescued were quite slim. The only traffic that would pass this way was rattly old farm trucks, and they probably came through here just once in a blue moon. Maybe a mail truck or a cyclist would show up. But where did they actually want to go? Where could they go?

"We'll try our best to reach Oskar's house." Markus seemed to read her mind. "Landweg 14, Wobbenbüll. I remember what Elise said. Perhaps he actually did hide a treasure somewhere around there. It's our only chance if we don't want to land in jail."

He was right. There were no other alternatives. Except to live out here in these woods and subsist on the squirrels and crows they could catch, until they died of appendicitis somewhere out in the brush. Their bodies with their maggot-cleaned eye sockets would be found a year later by some horrified mushroom hunter. At the thought of that, Tina almost found herself wishing for a clean jail cell and regular yard exercise.

"We weren't far from Husum and only three miles or so from Wobbenbüll when we got picked up," she said. A branch snapped across her leg as she ran, and she grimaced with pain.

"So we have to go back and get to the other side of Husum. It can't be all that far. We'll manage it."

Tina clenched her teeth. As they stepped out of the woods, they paused in the safety of the trees in case the police car was searching for them down this way.

"I hear something," she said. "An engine." She automatically moved back into the tree line.

"There!" Markus pointed into the distance, toward the end of the dusty lane. "Come out, it isn't a patrol car! It's a . . . You've got to be kidding! It's a Porsche." Markus pulled her toward the road. "Come on, let's try it. Maybe it'll stop."

"Why not?" Tina muttered, suddenly feeling completely dejected. "Porsche drivers are famous for picking up grubby-looking couples with dirty feet and twigs in their hair."

Markus didn't reply but stuck out his thumb as if he were eighteen and on his way on a summer trip.

To Tina's astonishment, the car slowed down and came to a stop in front of them. Someone rolled down the passenger-side window.

"Oskar?" Tina stared at him as if he were an apparition. "Is it really you? What the . . . ?"

"Jeez, you both look splendid. There's nothing more bracing than a refreshing stroll through the woods, is there?"

"How—"

"Don't look so flabbergasted. Viktoria and Elise got me away from those idiots."

At those words, Viktoria's head appeared next to Oskar's. She was sitting at the wheel and looked like she was having the time of her life.

"I called her," Oskar explained, "and Viktoria acted like she was my daughter and Elise was my ex-wife. A toast to the cluelessness of the county police! They didn't even notice us follow the patrol car that picked you up. All we had to do was wait and watch until you dashed into the woods. Lucky for us, we could see the track from where we were idling off the road, down from the rest area. And now get in before some forest ghost gets you. It's time for you to tell me all about your marvelous vacation stay at the precinct. And tomorrow morning, we'll all drive together to Wobbenbüll. It's time you saw my dream castle up close."

"But the car," Markus stammered. "Where did you . . . I mean, did you . . . ?"

"Don't worry. It isn't stolen. It belongs to Viktoria. I think it suits me better, though." Oskar proudly tapped on the dashboard. "You know that when an old dog starts to learn new tricks, nothing can stop him."

His laughter rang through the car.

18

They drove along the beat-up road back toward Husum without encountering anyone else, much less a police car. And even if one had appeared on the horizon, they wouldn't have attracted an officer's attention. Viktoria drove her speedster as if it were a stroller, and the tinted windows blocked any views into the interior of the Porsche. Tina slowly started to relax. Markus told Oskar and the two women how they had given Susi and her colleague the slip at the rest area, for which they earned Oskar's highest admiration.

Tina leaned back against Markus, who soothingly stroked her hair. Maybe everything would turn out all right in the end, even if she had no idea what their future life might look like. They were outlaws, criminals. Tina's unflattering drowned-corpse photo would forever stare out of police files around the country. They would have to spend the rest of their days in wigs and sunglasses and fake beards, always careful that nobody recognized them or had reason to check their IDs. They would never be able to hold real jobs, and there would be no pensions for them. In all likelihood, by the time she reached fifty-seven, Tina would be staggering around a shopping mall with an empty wine bottle, shouting obscenities at startled pedestrians, while Markus and his three-day beard would be sitting in front of their sleeping spot, accosting people with a slurred "Canya spare a euro?" Perhaps Tina would even have a cat or a hamster as a kindred spirit she could carry around in a tote bag, like the crazy old woman who lived close to them in Ingolstadt. And would they ever be reunited with Paul? She didn't want to think about that. That was impossible. Everyone knew that hope died last.

She gazed out the window, feeling exhausted, and saw Elise's mansion emerge out of the darkness.

~

"Home sweet home," Oskar trilled happily as they passed the sign for Wobbenbüll the next morning. He had been right; it truly was lovely and peaceful here. Small cottages, a few horses here and there, the sea in the distance. Tina wished she could trade places with the horses so she could spend the rest of her life grazing in this landscape.

"Oskar's house is up there around the corner," Elise told them as they drove past a couple of sheep on an endless expanse of green. The sheep didn't pay them the slightest bit of attention and happily munched on. "A gorgeous setting. You'll like it there."

Viktoria turned left at an intersection, and all of a sudden, they had a view of the open sea across the dike. On a whim, Tina opened her window and inhaled deeply. "Smell that, Markus. That fresh North Sea air."

"Close that window in the back!" Oskar cried. "The thumping makes my poor old ears pop. Besides, we're almost there, and then you can breathe in entire bucketloads of sea air."

"It looks great," Markus said.

"Doesn't it?" Oskar crowed as a dilapidated country house appeared before them. "All right, I admit that it isn't exactly a fairy-tale castle. But when the prince returns, all it needs is a little love and attention . . . Viktoria, stop! What in the world is that?"

Viktoria slowed down, and they all looked at the crooked sign that seemed to be holding on with its last dying strength to a post in front of the house. Meyer Realty, For Sale was printed in large, bold letters on it. A red arrow with a phone number was mounted beneath it. At that moment, it dawned on Tina that this ramshackle cottage had to be Oskar's house. And right after that, she realized that there was no way that a "treasure" could be hidden anywhere around here. The house, which stood like a rotten tooth in the midst of the immaculate North Sea landscape, had broken windowpanes with paint peeling from the frames like sunburnt skin and a door that was hanging askew from its hinges. Whatever had been inside and worth getting could have been removed at any time over the past few decades by anyone who had strolled past here on their way to the beach.

"My moron of a son-in-law has already put my home up for sale!" Oskar shouted. "But I'm still alive and kicking!"

"Okay, Mama, I think we need to head back." Viktoria cleared her throat. "There's something I have to take care of, and you should . . . yeah. Let's just go." Obviously, the sight of this collapsing ruin left even cosmopolitan Viktoria at a loss for what to do next.

"You can go." Elise didn't even look at her daughter. "I'll stay."

"But I don't think that's a good idea. The place looks dangerous."

"I said I'll stay."

Viktoria sighed. "Okay. Call me immediately if . . ."

The rest of the sentence hung unspoken in the air. Elise didn't respond anyway, and Viktoria shook her head.

"For sale, for sale," Oskar muttered grimly. "This is my parents' home, not a carton of fresh eggs. The house belongs to me. I belong in that house! Am I also up for sale? Buy that house and get an old man with it for half price. A weekend deal!"

Markus and Tina exchanged awkward looks with Viktoria and Elise.

"No rush, Viktoria," Elise said without taking her eyes off Oskar, who had struggled angrily out of the car and was now holding on to the roof of the Porsche.

"My wheelchair," he growled. "I refuse to crawl into my own home."

Tina hurriedly climbed out of the car, unfolded the wheelchair, and pushed it over to Oskar, who lowered himself into it. She then guided him over to what had once been an arguably handsome dwelling. Right beside the garden fence, under a large apple tree standing in front of the house, he signaled for Tina to stop. This had to be the tree Oskar had told them about, the one beneath which his dog was buried.

Tina felt her chest tighten. Oskar was sitting there in his wheelchair, just as crooked and slanting as his old house, his hand clamped around the rotten fence post. She closed her eyes for a moment. Regardless of the final outcome of all this, regardless of how desolate this place looked, Oskar had at least been able to see his home one last time. And that alone made everything worth it in the end. In her case, Tina couldn't imagine feeling nostalgic about their boring and overpriced apartment in a building full of busybodies and bores. She had never lived anywhere that had made her sad to leave. She had grown up in a gray apartment complex that had been built before World War II, where frustrated housewives had literally killed themselves to win the prize for the best polished landings and the smell of sauerkraut and floor polish had seeped into the pores of the building's residents. After that had come a shared apartment that smelled permanently of litter boxes, although no cat lived there, and where Tina's groceries, except for a jar of pickles, had mysteriously and regularly disappeared from the fridge. And then there had been the first apartment with Markus—a tiny studio apartment with a balcony, on which Tina had tried in vain to keep a couple of tomato plants alive. In light of all that, she almost envied Oskar his memories, regardless of how dilapidated his family home now looked.

Tina knew he needed consolation.

"Come on," she called to Markus. He got out of the car along with Elise. Viktoria gave a short honk and drove off, and Tina prepared herself emotionally to provide moral support to poor Oskar.

However, he turned his head over his shoulder and yelled, "Let's get going! It's time we dig up your reward, you rascals!"

"Dig up?" Markus asked slowly. He ran a finger weakly over the peeling paint on the fence, which swayed dangerously at the slightest touch.

"Yes, dig up. But don't worry, it's not my great-grandmother's skeleton," Oskar said, noticing Tina's startled look. "She's buried over in the Husum Cemetery. Next to her neighbor, by the way. They spent their whole lives arguing, and I bet they're still at it. Over who had the prettier flowers or got the most visitors or whose yard was raked better."

"Oskar, you actually have something hidden here?" Markus raised his eyebrows at Tina.

"Don't insult me! Of course I do. Do you really think I would have lured you up here with empty promises? Elise, tell them. I always keep my word."

"Oskar always keeps his word," Elise repeated with a flicker of amusement.

Oskar always keeps his word . . . Well, what were they waiting for? Tina reached for Markus's hand, and together, they trailed Oskar into the house as Elise pushed the wheelchair. Tina caught a glimpse of a living room with yellow flowered wallpaper and blue sprigged curtains, a room in which time seemed to have stood still. There was also a large eat-in kitchen with a bench and a tiled stove, as well as a view of the sea and a romantic, overgrown back garden. Everything was a little dusty and old fashioned but in a perfect location. That was beyond question. Whoever bought this house would be able to create something idyllic.

"It's in the kitchen," Oskar explained, as he took a short breather by the stove. "You'll have to pull up a few floorboards, Markus. Can you manage that?"

"Of course. What am I looking for, exactly?"

"A flat metal box. It originally held Christmas tree decorations, if I recall rightly. Christmas balls and such."

Tina felt a twinge of disappointment. An ornament box? Christmas balls weren't usually all that big, and a box like that couldn't hold that much. She had secretly been hoping for something the size of a suitcase. Or at least a duffel bag stuffed with bills.

Oskar rolled himself over to the kitchen table. "It's under this. The one board is a little higher than the others. It was always like that. Drove my mother crazy because the table always wobbled. After my parents died, I discovered that there was a cavity underneath it, presumably built by a previous owner. Goodness knows what they had hidden in it. Maybe their money, maybe love letters, maybe just their canned goods. When I found the hole, all it held was a dead spider." He turned toward them. "Anyway, get cracking. I think there might be some tools still around here. I can help you too."

"Absolutely not," Elise interjected. "You won't be scooting all around on the floor. You may come with me, and we'll take a walk."

"But I have to see if it is still there," Oskar objected. "I have waited decades for this moment."

"This might take a while," said Markus, trying in vain to work the boards free with a small screwdriver. "This is all I have. I need to find something else, like a pickax or something."

"See?" Elise smiled at Oskar. "Markus needs some time. And you need some fresh air, my love. Just enjoy the seaside. After all, you could still be stuck at the hospital, waiting on your family."

"She's right, as usual. I should be grateful that I can once again spend time on the beach with a beautiful woman, while my son-in-law enjoys the finer services of some mental institution." Oskar squeezed Elise's hand gently as she reached for the wheelchair handles.

Tina watched the two of them as they slowly moved toward the beach.

"He's just so happy with her," she said to Markus.

"And she with him."

"They were meant to be together."

"I think they know that. It's rare. They are lucky."

There was a little awkward silence. Tina didn't know what to say. "Do you honestly want to search for Oskar's treasure?" She finally maneuvered the conversation into safer grounds.

"Why not? Oskar said there's something hidden down there. You don't believe him?"

Tina didn't know what to say. She actually didn't believe anything was down there. She didn't believe, because nothing in her life had ever turned out great. Then again, she did believe, because she believed in Oskar. He wouldn't lie to them—why would he?

"Why don't you go for a walk too? Nobody's around here, so we don't need to hide."

"Okay." A stroll along a lonely stretch of beach sounded quite appealing, especially after all she had been through the past few days. Breathing in the fresh sea air and all that. On the other hand, she didn't want to leave Markus on his own. What if the cop with the mullet showed up because Susi had gotten cold feet and confessed everything? Maybe someone had found out that Oskar still owned a house here. Or what if a curious neighbor stopped by, attracted by the noise, only to find Markus yanking up the kitchen floor? Then her short foray into freedom would be quickly over.

"Go on," Markus encouraged her. "And by the time you get back, I'll have found a Christmas box stuffed full of money."

"Hopefully," Tina said. "Hopefully it won't just be mummified gingerbread cookies baked by Elise a long time ago that Oskar kept for sentimental reasons." With that, she stepped outside.

~

She followed the narrow path down to the sea. The tide had left its mark in the sand, having lured the water back out to sea. Soon it would be driving that same water back up onto the shore. The sun stood high in the sky, but fortunately a gentle breeze tempered the heat. Tina studied the beach. She was walking on the seabed, so to speak. What a strange thought! She bent down to look for little crabs and shells. Although she didn't see any, she caught sight of damp wheelchair tracks and footprints on the boardwalk. Oskar and Elise must have passed this way. Where were they? Tina glanced around. A small group of white beach chairs were clustered farther along the beach. Two families with small children had taken possession of them. Tina could see beach pails and an inflatable crocodile as the smell of sunscreen wafted across to her.

She listened. There was nothing to hear except for the chattering of the children, the whoosh of the sea, and the clattering of a horse-drawn carriage on the other side of the levee.

Far off on the edge of the horizon, she could make out a small fishing boat and, next to it, a daredevil windsurfer. There was no way that Oskar was either on the boat or on the surfboard, so Tina focused back on the wheelchair track. There, up at the end of the boardwalk, something was sitting. As she drew closer, she realized it was the wheelchair. It was sitting there empty; Oskar and Elise were nowhere to be seen. Tina stopped, puzzled. Where were the two of them? Footprints led straight from the wheelchair to the edge of the water. Tina's heart started to pound faster. The tide would turn in less than an hour, and everything that was here on the beach would be engulfed by water.

"Oskar?" Tina shouted. "Elise?"

No answer. Tina pushed the wheelchair along uncertainly, before folding it up. She kept calling their names. Was that a distant cry? She started to run. These mudflats held dangers. They had to know that! Why had they left the wheelchair behind?

She hurried along the tracks, which ran about a hundred yards toward the water. But then they took an abrupt turn. Thank God. Tina strode on, continuing to follow the tracks, which led to a group of sea buckthorn bushes at the top of the dunes. The tracks stopped here. She now heard voices and laughter.

"Oskar?" This time, she saw them. They were walking slowly next to each other as Elise held Oskar's arm.

"We're practicing, Tina." Oskar sounded excited. "We're practicing walking. Elise thinks that, if I practice every day, I won't need my old fiery chariot much longer. Look how far we've already gone!"

"That's great!" Tina shook her head in a mixture of joy and concern. It was astonishing what the presence of a good woman could achieve. Oskar looked electrified; his gait seemed downright buoyant. "For a moment, I thought the North Sea had swallowed you both up. Here's your wheelchair."

"Ah, thanks. But I would've fetched it myself eventually." Despite Oskar's dismissive tone, sweat was beading on his forehead. "Was Markus able to get the boards up?"

"I don't know," Tina admitted. "Come back with me, and we can see."

They strolled leisurely back to the house, and Tina glanced at Elise with gratitude. "Oskar, you seem to have found a new lease on life. The sea air really can work wonders." She exchanged a look with the older woman.

"It does, doesn't it?" Elise replied. "It's as if he were ninety again."

"Hey! I just turned eighty-seven," Oskar protested.

"Oh, that's right." Elise bumped him playfully in the side, and Tina thought the two of them suited each other marvelously. Why hadn't they gotten together many years ago? Because Elise had let herself get blinded by another man's money?

"I feel wonderful." Oskar got up. "So good that I even feel capable of getting rid of this trash myself." And with that, he gave the for-sale sign in front of his house a kick. At this unexpected attack, the post snapped and fell over with a crash.

"And that's that. As of today, it's no longer for sale," Oskar said contentedly. He pulled a thermos out of Elise's bag. "Who would like some tea? We also brought cookies along."

"Me." Tina could think of nothing better right now. And then she walked ahead of them to see how far Markus had gotten.

"Markus? Do you want some tea?" She pushed the wheelchair into the front hall. "Guess what? Elise has been practicing walking with Oskar, and she thinks that he won't need his wheelchair much—" She broke off.

Markus was standing in the middle of the kitchen. Next to him, a pickax was leaning against the wall, and at his feet, the boards were pulled up. He was holding a flat, rusty box. It wasn't much bigger than a shoebox. He shot Tina a strange look.

"What is it, Markus? What's in the box?"

Markus wiped his forehead, exhausted. "Promise me you won't get upset. We'll figure things out, I swear. We'll find . . . we'll find a solution. I won't screw up the next holdup. Or there doesn't even have to be another holdup. We can get jobs somewhere, where nobody'll turn us in. We'll earn a little money, and it'll be enough to live on. We—"

Tina clenched her hands into fists. "What is in the box, Markus?"

19

Instead of answering, Markus flipped up the box lid.

Tina took a step forward to take a look. No bills. That was the first thing that flashed through her mind. Dammit, there was no money. There were also no pieces of jewelry, no pearls, no family silver, nothing except . . .

"Old photographs?" she managed to say. "Oskar's old family photos? He hid them down there?" She couldn't believe it. Why was fate so cruel to them? As if on autopilot, she reached for the topmost picture. A black-and-white photo, very professional looking. You could have almost called it artistic. It showed an extremely pretty woman with long blond hair and large eyes rimmed with unbelievably long eyelashes, which gave her a doll-like air. Her clothes looked like they were from the sixties—minidress, long crocheted vest, and knee-high boots. She was sitting on the bottom step of a broad staircase in front of some aristocratic home as she smiled into the camera. The next photo showed her hand in hand with a bearded man in a hippie outfit. Who the devil was this? Oskar's aunt, cousin, ballroom dance lesson partner?

"Family photos," Tina repeated in disbelief as she let go of the picture. It sailed onto the kitchen floor. She struggled against a desire to stomp on it.

"There's a photo album in the box. All the pictures are of people from the sixties. I only glanced at them. And then there are a few loose photos. That's it. I'm really sorry," Markus whispered.

"It's not your fault," Tina said, still on autopilot. "Not your fault." She covered her face with her hands, doing her best to not break down and cause a scene. But that was exactly what she felt like doing. Crap, crap, crap! Now what? What were they going to do now? They couldn't stay in this dilapidated place, where the North Sea wind whistled through every crack and broken windowpane. They had to acquire money from somewhere. *Acquire.* God, not that! She had to—

"Ah, he actually found it!" Oskar's cheerful voice crowed behind her. "Excellent, my boy. Did you take a look? I bet you didn't expect that, did you?" Supported by Elise, Oskar sat down on one of the kitchen chairs.

What was the old man going on about? Was he making fun of them? Despite everything, Tina couldn't believe that of him.

"No. We didn't really expect to find your family photos," she finally croaked.

"It's great that you can have them back again," Markus jumped in, although his voice faltered in his disappointment. "They'll help you relive your memories, and we're glad we could help you with that, of course—"

"Are you completely nuts?" Oskar asked in astonishment. "Did you even look at the pictures?"

"Yes, a few, but not all of them," Tina lied. "The woman there, she's really pretty. An old girlfriend of yours?" She pointed at the photo on the floor and leaned down to pick it up.

"Stop, stop! Hold it by the edges!" Oskar sounded extremely nervous. "And don't get any spots on it. Why isn't that one in the sleeve with the rest of them?"

He cautiously took the photo away from the baffled Tina, as if it could explode at any moment. "You have no idea who this is?"

"No, how would I?" Tina asked, astonished. She peeked over at Markus for help, then let her eyes wander across the old-fashioned kitchen and the hole in the floor before they finally came to rest on Elise. "Is this perhaps you, Elise?"

Oskar rolled his eyes. "Young people these days really don't have a clue, despite the fact they spend all their time online. The entire span of human knowledge is available on their phones, and what do they do? They exchange recipes and cat photos!" Oskar made grumbling sounds for a few seconds, then pointed triumphantly at the picture. "That, my dears, is Pattie Boyd."

"Who?" Tina and Markus asked in unison.

"George Harrison's wife," Oskar declared. "Now, please, don't tell me you have no idea who he is!"

"George Harrison? You mean, as in the Beatles?" Markus stared at Oskar.

"Yes, or do you happen to know of anyone else named George Harrison? I don't. This shot is of the two of them together, George and Pattie." Oskar fished the other photo out of the box, the one of the blond woman with the bearded man. "They had just gotten married. Paul McCartney was their witness, by the way. Yes, that McCartney. Where is he, anyway . . . ? Just a sec. Here." He carefully picked up another photo and held it up to Tina's face. Literally. She recognized this face immediately, despite the fact that it looked extremely young in the picture. Paul McCartney in a light-colored trench coat on a terrace somewhere, with a neatly manicured English lawn and an oak-lined avenue in the background. He was shielding his eyes with his hand, as if he were facing the sun.

Oskar crooned a Beatles song softly. "And here's one of Eric. Clapton, I mean, before you ask me who that is. He married pretty Pattie later on, after she had broken up with George. Too much alcohol and cocaine, if you want to believe the tabloids. But here at their home in Henley-on-Thames, they were still happy. A beautiful estate. You would've liked it. No pesky neighbors, far and wide."

"Eric Clapton?" Markus repeated slowly. He now set the box down gingerly on the table.

"Yes, him. You know the song 'Wonderful Tonight,' don't you? Do you young people actually know anything anymore?"

"Of course I know it," Markus said. He promptly began to sing along with Clapton, albeit off-key.

Tina exchanged an amused look with Elise. Markus had spent his entire life convinced that the world had missed out on an amazing singer, as far as he was concerned.

"Uh, that's very nice, Markus." Oskar cut him short. "That song is about Pattie here and her long blond hair." He carefully pulled out another photo from the pile and held it up. "And here, you'll recognize him. Please tell me, for God's sake, that you know who this is." Oskar glared at them all defiantly.

"Mick Jagger," Tina, Markus, and Elise said in unison.

The photo showed the singer in a completely atypical pose, neither as a highly styled bad boy with pouty lips nor as the rocker with his guitar. This photo was of him sitting at a table in a café, absorbed in a book with the trace of a smile on his face.

"That's on King's Road in Chelsea, in London. I think it was 1968. He was waiting on Marianne Faithfull. Not long after that, he bought a house in Chelsea for fifty thousand pounds or so. These days, you can't even get a year-long pass at a parking garage in that neighborhood for that." Oskar shook his head. "Keith Richards bought a place just a few doors down from him. I photographed him, too, if I remember rightly. I think it was inside his home, so you'll get to see what it looked like in there. I didn't really share his taste, though, to be honest. Too many knickknacks and thick rugs. To each his own, but Keith was really nice during the shoot, no two ways about it."

And now the other shoe dropped. "You took all these pictures yourself?" Tina asked in disbelief.

"Of course, who else? Margaret Thatcher in her early days?" Oskar chortled at his own joke. "I told you about my career as a photographer when we were talking about good old Cher, God bless her soul. Oh wait, she's still alive!" Oskar started laughing again. "Where is everyone's sense of humor? Elise, you at least should be laughing with me."

The three stared at him, speechless. Tina nervously twisted her hair around her finger, while Markus rubbed his hands on his pants. Elise merely cocked one elegant eyebrow.

"Okay, maybe not," Oskar continued. "Anyway, I should at least tell you that these are all rather valuable unpublished original photos. Nobody has ever seen them. You're the first. I took these back in the day—the newspapers only ever wanted one, not a hundred, so these are the rest of them."

"But I don't understand—why didn't you sell them years ago?" Markus was the first to find his tongue again. "You could've made a fortune from them."

"You're right. But now they'll bring even more money. Now they'll bring *you* even more money." Oskar rapped his knuckles against the tin box.

"You never told me about these," Elise said. "Why not?"

"Because I was mad at you." His voice was tinged with bitterness. "You know why, and because I swore to myself that my criminal career was going to be just as spectacular as Helmut's. So that one day I could win you back, once I was swimming in money. But life somehow got in the way. You had your life here, and I had mine with my wife in Ingolstadt. We had a daughter then, and, well, the rest is history. These photos were supposed to be my safeguard. Deep down, I knew that at some point in time these would come into play. And then when Bonnie and Clyde of the Ingolstadt Brotherhood kidnapped me, I had a feeling this was my last chance." Oskar fell silent.

Elise gently laid her hand on his arm, and Tina swallowed. She needed to process all this.

"How many photos are there?" Markus asked. He had always been the pragmatic one.

"You mean, how much are they worth, right? You rogue." Oskar winked and rubbed his hands together. In his new T-shirt, he looked like a joyful carpenter about to get to work on his demolished kitchen. "I think we should leave that to my dear Elise's antiques dealer. But I'm pretty sure that you'll get more than a thousand euros for them. Little tip—most of them are autographed."

~

Back at Elise's house, Tina downed a glass of whiskey that Markus poured for her. Her hands didn't stop trembling, though. If she wanted to be honest, she was scared. Scared that any minute the village cop would stick his badly styled head through the door and shout, "Gotcha!" Scared that for some reason the pictures weren't real or weren't worth anything. Scared that her own courage wouldn't hold, because if everything turned out to be true and the skinny antiques dealer with the pencil mustache, who was now sitting with Elise in the living room and inspecting the photos, gave them a sum, Tina and Markus would have to decide what they would do next. However, at that very moment, all she wanted to do was remain stretched out on Elise's couch in the guest room for the rest of her days, listening to the seagulls and having tea brought to her every few hours. It dawned on Tina that, most likely, she was just completely worn out.

She heard babbling voices from the living room but couldn't make out any distinct words. Markus stood at the door and pressed his ear against it.

"Can you hear anything?" Tina asked. "What's the man saying?"

"Don't know. Gosh, I wish I could go out there and just ask him."

"No, we're supposed to stay in here. Elise told us to. Or do you want to get caught when we're so close to the finish line? We're criminals on the run, and last night, we cuffed an officer to a pipe in a filthy restroom. Don't forget about that."

"What?" Markus stared at her for a moment, uncomprehending. "Oh, of course. I had actually forgotten about that. There's too much going on. And as for Susi . . ." He shook his head. "Who would've guessed that she would save our skins?"

"It was really brave of her." Tina nodded. "I hope she won't get fired. But I honestly never would've thought Susi had it in her. You can never truly see into a person's soul. I wish I had spent more time with her over the last few years. Deep down, I knew she was miserable."

Loud laughter now floated over from the living room. They both looked at the door.

"Why are they laughing?" Markus asked, instantly nervous. "Is it all a joke?"

Tina stood up and walked over to the window to look down into the garden. She paused. "Markus, don't panic."

Stepping away from the door, he paced the room restlessly. He came to a stop when he reached the desk on which a computer was sitting. "Why didn't I think about that before? eBay! Let's take a look on there and see how much a photo like one of those is worth!" He raised the screen on the laptop. "Password required," he muttered. "Crap. Should've thought of that too. Let's think. There were at least a hundred photos in the album, another twenty or thirty loose in the sleeve . . . Help me do the math, Tina."

"Markus, stop! How am I supposed to calculate anything if I don't even know what one of them is worth?"

"Then just guess!"

"Guess?! Tell me how I'm supposed to—" Tina stopped mid-sentence. They were about to start arguing, and how dumb would that be? It was just stress. Immense stress, the tension they were under. She suddenly felt laughter bubbling up inside her. The longer she watched Markus, the more the corners of her mouth twitched. He was staring at her in bewilderment, and his glasses were slipping askew again. They had grown looser during the excitement of the past few days.

"Markus . . ." Tina started laughing so hard she got the hiccups. "Regardless of how much the photos are worth, the first thing we're going to buy is a pair of decent glasses for you."

"What?" Markus asked, totally lost. "Why do I need new glasses?"

"Because as of today, you're a rich man, my boy." Oskar had slipped into the room unnoticed. He was holding on to the doorframe and grinning at the two of them. "And rich men usually dress elegantly. Unless his name happens to be Bill Gates, or he has a preference for flannel shirts." And then Oscar named a figure with so many zeros that Tina forgot to breathe, and her hiccups vanished as quickly as they had appeared.

20

"Is that him?" Tina peered cautiously through the curtains to the street. They had been waiting for about a week on this ominous Martin, an old friend of Oskar's. The latter had described him as "a man with the best connections." He was the second stranger in whose hands they had placed their fate, so to speak. The first had been the goateed antiques dealer who had made off with the photographs after promising to "take care of everything."

Tina could hardly take it. This was worse than being grounded as a child or getting seriously sick during the summer break when everyone else was going on vacation. They were not allowed to leave the house, since the danger was too great that someone might recognize them. Their escape from the rest area had given rise to all sorts of new sensational headlines. Gangster Couple Escapes Again!, How Incompetent Is Our Police Force?, and Brutal Torture of Police Officer were a few of the most innocuous ones. They'd even caught sight of the mullet cop on TV, though he hadn't had anything much to say.

"He looks a little too old," Markus replied. They watched as a tall, white-haired man approached the house. "Oskar said that Martin is a 'young whippersnapper.'"

"Young compared to Oskar, maybe. I bet that's our guy." She pointed at the man, who was now striding briskly toward the front door. A few seconds later, a melodic doorbell sounded.

“Martin, you old goat!” they heard Oskar call out, and they both stepped into the living room and joined the two men as they thumped each other boisterously on the shoulder. “You look as young as ever!” Oskar’s ring of white hair stood out wildly from his head, but he was wearing a blue-striped polo shirt. Elise had obviously gone shopping for him.

“At least younger than you,” the man shot back with a laugh. He held his hand out to Tina and Markus. “It always makes him mad that he’s a few years older than me.”

“Nonsense,” Oskar said. “We’re both old geezers, even if you are only eighty-two. One or the other of us will be the first to kick the bucket, but in the meantime, I need you to take care of something for us. These two are—”

“I know who they are.” Martin gave a dismissive wave. “I keep myself informed. Neat, what all you managed to pull off. Not bad.”

“Thanks,” Tina peeped.

“And taking away the cop chick’s gun and locking her up in the bathroom—kudos to you.” Martin laughed loudly.

Tina squirmed, embarrassed. Oskar had been so impressed with their escape from the patrol car that they simply hadn’t gotten around to telling him about Susi’s assistance. And maybe it wasn’t a bad idea if this secret remained between them and Susi.

“Ladies.” Martin gave a little bow as Elise and Viktoria stepped into the room. He then set his small briefcase on the table. “So, the first thing we need are new passport photos. The last ones weren’t really all that flattering, were they?”

Tina flushed darkly. He actually was well informed.

“Don’t worry. Uncle Martin will take care of everything. Let’s get to work!” He rubbed his hands together. “Here is the plan.”

~

“Marion?” A few days later, Tina was using her new phone. “Please tell me you aren’t still sitting around at Fashion World.”

"Good Lord . . . it really is you! Everybody's still talking about you around here! Did you know that people follow your life on TikTok? Where in the world are you?"

Marion still didn't get it. Tina sighed.

"Marion, I can't tell you where I am. You know why. I just wanted to tell you goodbye. We . . ." Tina cleared her throat. "We're moving. And someday, Marion—listen to me—someday you'll get a postcard. Do you understand? And it will be from someone you don't know. And that'll be me."

"But I know you."

Please, God. "Yes, but I'll be using a different name. Got it?"

"Ah, okay. A postcard from where?"

"I don't know. But it will have a name and phone number on it, and then you can call me, okay?"

"Okay." Marion gulped. "And then you'll get me out?"

"Marion, the only one who can do that is you. No one can force you to work for Fashion World."

Marion was silent for a moment, and in the background, Tina caught Müller's voice, who was obviously being driven to the limits of her good upbringing by an especially annoying customer. "I'm really terribly sorry," Tina heard her say. "But I can't just wave a magic wand and make those pants in navy blue appear. They're sold out."

"You're right. No one can force me to be here." Marion sighed. "When are you . . . moving?"

"The day after tomorrow." Tina felt her chest tighten. After just sitting around for over a week and waiting, everything seemed to suddenly be happening at lightning speed.

"I wish you all the best." Marion's voice trembled a bit. "And don't forget about me! And one more thing. How will I know if the card is from you?"

"You'll know. It will mention something really awful, something neither one of us will ever forget."

"A corduroy blazer in chartreuse," Marion replied like a shot.

They both laughed, and Tina quickly hung up to keep from getting too emotional. She hurried to dial the next number. As she held her breath, she twirled her wedding ring. Everything needed to go just right now.

"Paul?" she whispered. "Did you get everything?"

"Yes. It's all just fine."

"You still have time to think about it."

"There's nothing to think about. Amelie broke up with me anyway, and Ottwald keeps babbling on and on about how my music is too loud. The apartment manager sent you an eviction notice, and I haven't liked school since the day you sent me to kindergarten."

"Ah, Paulie." Tina saw her son in her mind. Fingers crossed, everything would go smoothly. If it didn't go well, she would never forgive herself. She just needed to keep the faith. "See you in a few days, Paulie."

"See you then, Mom."

~

Tina was helping Elise set the table for their last supper together. However, she couldn't concentrate and kept dropping things, so Elise sent her out to keep Oskar company. He was sitting in a lounge chair on the terrace, happily watching the garden.

"Isn't it beautiful here?" he said. "Come on, join me."

Tina sat down on another of the loungers. "Oskar," she started tentatively, because one question had been bothering her for the past few days. "Oskar, why are you giving us all the money? I mean, it's a stunning sum, and you originally told us you were going to share the money with us. You could afford to have a grand life. You could restore your parents' house and live there with Elise. You could maybe travel a little, once you get more steady on your feet. You could—"

"I have everything I need," Oskar interrupted her gently, but firmly. A fresh evening breeze played around them, and the sun sat low on the horizon. "I got the love of my life back, although it's a damn shame old Helmut isn't around to see it. And I've found my way back home, and in my last few months, I'll be able to listen to the seagulls as I fall asleep, and not the farts and whiffles of some roommate at the nursing home. That's something."

"What did you say?" Tina felt her blood run cold. "What you do you mean, *last few months*?"

Oskar scooted a little closer to her. "Ah, my girl, my old ticker's playing out." He gave his chest a tap. "Heart disease. It's been in decline for years now. They told me it'll just give out sometime soon. But at least it's my arteries that are calcified and not my brain, right?" He started to laugh.

Tina didn't laugh with him. She couldn't believe what he had said. "Then . . . then what they said on the news about you was true? You actually do have a heart condition?" She remembered the incident at the wedding, when Oskar's face had drained of all color, and he had looked as if he had passed out in his wheelchair. He could have died there, right in front of them!

"Ah, the dumb reporters. They don't know what they're talking about half the time. They said I'm ninety and that there's life on Mars and that beer is unhealthy. Who knows what else! My heart will hold out a little longer." He gazed into the distance for a moment, sunk in thought, then turned his eyes, warm and affectionate, back on Tina. "But not long enough for me to blow all that money, and that's why you're getting it. After all, as they say, you can't take it with you. And if you don't have it, my stinker of a son-in-law will end up with it. Anyway, I'm so incredibly happy right now. And those who are happy shouldn't keep trying to become even happier."

"But, Oskar, will we . . . ?" Tears welled up in Tina's eyes. She couldn't finish the question she had started.

"I don't know if we will see each other again," Oskar said with a small smile. "Unless your airplane doesn't make it to its destination, in which case our paths might cross much sooner than expected."

"Oskar, don't talk like that!" Tina couldn't keep her composure. She wrapped her arms around the old man's neck and howled like a newborn. "Why didn't you tell us? We could've . . . we could've . . ."

Oskar gently patted her back to comfort her. "What would you have done, hmm? You would've driven me to a hospital, and that would've been the end of our road trip. Right?"

"Yes," Tina admitted between sobs.

"Exactly. Besides, you were both already as jumpy as cats on a hot tin roof. You would've lost your nerve and shot me in the leg or something."

"Oskar." Tina laughed through her tears. "The pistol wasn't real."

"That's what they all say afterward." Oskar cocked a knowing eyebrow. "But seriously, you helped me more than anyone has in the past twenty years. And for that, I am eternally grateful to you."

"And we are eternally grateful to you too." Tina wiped the tears off her face. "I don't know how we are going to manage without you now."

"Of course you will manage. You are clever and full of good ideas, and Markus—he's the perfect gangster in the making. Still a bit impulsive, but he's got promise." He reached for her hand and squeezed it.

"You think so?"

"I do. And you have each other. That is half the battle. No, it's the entire battle." With that, he leaned back in his chair and gazed up at the sky, where the sun blazed red one last time before slipping below the horizon a few seconds later without a trace.

21

Tina did a double take every time she spotted herself in the mirrored glass wall across from Gate A6. The woman in the elegant gray pantsuit and large tinted glasses looked vastly different from the Tina Michel she had known for the past forty-five years. And that wasn't just because of the freshly dyed blond hair and the costly necklace she was wearing, a gift from Elise. The woman in the glass wall looked like a carefree, wealthy tourist who was waiting, a little impatiently, for her flight number to be called so that she could finally put her feet up and enjoy a glass of champagne in her business-class seat.

She reached into her purse and pulled out the postcards she had purchased earlier from a souvenir shop. One of them showed a grinning garden gnome in front of a windmill. It was for Susi, as a thank-you and a little hint that they had made it. Even without a note on it, Susi would understand. The other card showed a beach with a hammock strung between two palm trees, similar to the ones awaiting them at their destination. This was for Marion. Tina planned to post both cards as soon as they arrived.

From the duty-free shop across the way wafted a mélange of various aftershaves and perfumes from all over the world, thanks to the fact that bored travelers sprayed the stuff around like insecticides. For the umpteenth time, Tina wondered who in the world would actually purchase a three-thousand-euro Christian Dior purse right before takeoff, like others might buy a newspaper. Rich women. Just like her, she realized suddenly. The reality still hadn't sunk in, and she didn't think it would until she was sitting on the plane.

She flipped through the pages of her magazine but could hardly concentrate, because her thoughts kept turning to Oskar. And to everything she was about to leave behind. Every time she envisioned Oskar's face with its wreath of white hair and the laugh lines around his eyes, as she had seen them just this morning when he had hugged her one last time, her throat tightened.

She stood up and joined Paul and Markus, who were lingering in front of a small café in the departure area. *Almost like before,* Tina thought. As if they still needed to count every cent and consider whether they could afford to go in there or if coffee in a to-go cup was their best option.

"Afraid to go in?" she asked. "Come on, my treat." She pushed them toward one of the open tables. "Coffee? Or water? Or what about champagne?" She beamed at Markus.

"Cappuccino. I don't want any bubbly until we're safely back on the ground," Markus replied, nervously fingering his boarding pass.

"You and your fear of flying!" Paul teased, though he sounded concerned as well.

Tina walked over to the bar to place their order. A server with dark circles under her eyes was dashing back and forth. The espresso machine needed cleaning, used glasses were sitting around, and several patrons were waiting impatiently, following her every move with glares like poison arrows.

The server struggled desperately with the espresso machine and called out over her shoulder, "What would you like to order?" A man in a polo shirt rattled off an order for at least seven people, and the server nodded and gave a stressed smile. Tina wondered how in the world anyone could remember all of that. She caught sight of a photo pinned to the wall behind the cash register. It showed a little boy standing next to a snowman as he laughed proudly into the camera. This had to be the son of the server; they both had the same black curls. The picture reminded Tina of a photo she had kept for years on her desk at Fashion World, as if it were a monument to freedom. In that photo, a small, four-year-old Paul was sitting on a blanket in a summer meadow, a lake glittering in the background. The sight of this photo had always given Tina strength whenever she faced a day that seemed to stretch on forever. She had daydreamed about summertime and almost believed she could smell the meadow and the water instead of the cheese and crackers from Müller's desk.

Tina studied the annoyed looks on the faces of the other customers in the mirror behind the bar.

"Will we get our orders sometime today?" someone loudly complained, and a few other guests murmured in agreement. The server bravely kept her cheerful expression and tried to move her hands quicker. "Here you go." She set an espresso down in front of the man in the polo shirt.

"No, I wanted an espresso macchiato," he complained instantly.

Tina was 100 percent sure that he had ordered a regular espresso. She could tell that working here as a server was about as bad as working for Fashion World.

The woman in front of Tina also had something to criticize. "My coffee is extremely hot. I could've burnt my tongue!" she protested.

Her companion remarked just as loudly, "See, I told you we should've gotten something to drink in the lounge."

Tina watched the two women as they stalked away. "That would've been better for everyone, wouldn't it?" She smiled at the server. "Anyway, three cappuccinos, please." With that, she stuck twenty euros into the tip cup on the counter, which was empty except for a lonely fifty-cent coin. As she walked off with the drinks, she thought that Oskar would've done the very same thing.

~

After setting the drinks in front of Paul and Markus, Tina sat down with them.

"You really don't want anything to eat, Paul?" she asked. She had been mothering him nonstop ever since he had rejoined them. But Paul only shot her a warning look. "Florian, I mean. You don't want anything to eat, Florian? What about you . . . Matthias?" She looked at Markus.

"No, Lisa." Markus tried to keep a straight face.

Tina thought they sounded like the first lesson in some beginner's German textbook. It would take a while for them to get used to their new names.

"Hey, look at that!" Markus pointed at the screen mounted on the wall, on which a headline scrolled slowly underneath a blond CNN reporter: "Newly discovered original photos of the Beatles, the Stones, and other musicians from the Swinging Sixties sell for over two million pounds at Sotheby's!"

"Pinch me!" Tina whispered back. "That's twice as much as Oskar guessed."

"I think he suspected it." Markus couldn't take his eyes off the screen. "He didn't want to overwhelm us."

Tina nodded and imagined the small old man sitting in front of the TV. Overjoyed, he would put his arm around Elise and tell her that he wouldn't have needed all that cash anyway—after all, you couldn't take it with you to the pearly gates. Or he'd toss off one of his usual quips, the kind Tina wished she had jotted down, just as much as she wished that she had met Oskar much earlier in her life.

"I need to go to the bathroom." Paul stood up.

"Sure. I've heard that the fear of flying can be hereditary." Markus poked him in the leg.

"Stop, Dad." Paul rolled his eyes. "I'll be right back."

Tina watched her son as he strolled off coolly, as if he caught flights every day. The three of them were finally together. On their way to a better future. She snuggled up to Markus. "Do you know how happy I am right now? I can't recall the last time I was so happy. A new life is waiting for us. A second chance. And there's no one I'd rather start over with than you." She kissed him. "You're the best."

He put his arm around her. "And I can't think of anyone I would rather spend the rest of my life with than you. I'm so glad you aren't mad at me anymore."

"It really wasn't your fault. You did what you did because you loved us so much. And I thank you for that—even if what you did was totally insane." She patted his cheek. "We've been amazingly fortunate in our lives, don't you think?"

"You can say that again. Things could have turned out quite differently."

"That's not what I mean. We were really lucky that we ever found each other. Not everyone gets that." She couldn't help thinking about Susi.

"Yes, that's true." He looked at her, his eyes full of affection. "I don't want to imagine what would've happened if someone else had gotten to you first."

"Or the other way around." She kissed him again. "Another woman wouldn't have appreciated your guitar playing as much."

"Just you wait. The first thing I'm going to do when we get there is buy myself a new guitar, and then we'll go down to the beach, and—"

"Does Dad plan to start a band?" Paul had returned.

"No, I—"

The airport speaker system crackled to life.

"Final boarding call for the flight to Miami. Please come to Gate A6 for boarding."

"That's us!" Markus jumped to his feet and knocked over his empty cup.

Tina got up too. "It's time to go, Schmidts. Come on! First stop, Miami, and then on to George Town!" They strolled unhurriedly over to Gate A6, where an overly cheerful gate agent scanned their boarding passes and wished them a good flight.

"I bet they build a ton of boats on the Cayman Islands," she heard Markus say quietly to Paul from behind her.

Tina didn't hear Paul's response because, at that moment, her phone rang. She answered it and immediately recognized Oskar's voice.

"The money's been transferred," he announced happily. "It's a bit more than we thought. I hope you don't mind."

"Thank you, Oskar. We—"

"And I wanted to tell you one last thing," he interrupted her. "For heaven's sake, get yourselves a real gun in George Town, all right? You'll need it if you want them to take you seriously down there."

Tina held back a smile. "We'll do that, Oskar. I promise."

"Be sure to pass that along to Marko."

"Markus."

"I know, I know." Tina could've sworn that at that moment she heard a soft chuckle on the other end of the line. "Just wanted to make sure you were really listening."

ABOUT THE AUTHOR

Ulrike Herwig grew up in Jena, Germany. She is the award-winning author of numerous novels for adults and children, and she writes under multiple pen names. Her work has been translated into more than ten languages. She studied English and German and lived in London for almost ten years, where she also worked as a teacher for a while. In 2002, she moved to Seattle, where she now lives with her family.

ABOUT THE TRANSLATOR

Rachel Reynolds has translated more than twenty works, including *Forty Hours* by Kathrin Lange, *Love Letters from Montmartre* by Nicolas Barreau, and *Place of No Return* by Andrea C. Hoffmann and Mihrigul Tursun. She was one of the founders of the Global Literature in Libraries Initiative, which aims to broaden the audience for world literature and translation. She lives in Tennessee with her family.